TORCHWOOD

TRACE
MEMORY

D0388212

The *Torchwood* series from BBC Books:

TORCHWOOD
TRACE
MEMORY

David Llewellyn

BBC BOOKS

2 4 6 8 10 9 7 5 3 1

First published in 2008 by BBC Books, an imprint of Ebury Publishing
A Random House Group company. This paperback edition published 2013.

Torchwood is a BBC Wales production for BBC Two
Executive Producers: Russell T Davies and Julie Gardner
Co-producer: Chris Chibnall
Series Producer: Richard Stokes

The Random House Group Limited Reg. No. 954009.
Addresses for companies within the Random House Group can be found at
www.randomhouse.co.uk.

A CIP catalogue record for this book is available from the British Library.

ISBN 9781849907149

Commissioning Editor: Albert DePetrillo
Series Editor: Steve Tribe
Production Controller: Phil Spencer

Cover design by Lee Binding @ Tea Lady © BBC 2008
Typeset in Albertina and Century Gothic
Printed and bound in the USA

November 1953

It was a foggy night in Tiger Bay. The moon, jaundiced by the fumes of industry, reflected like a shimmering penny in the black sea of the channel, while the fog-smothered silhouettes of warehouses stood out like tombstones against the night sky.

It was a cold night, too, and the four of them shuffled from foot to foot and clapped their gloved hands together in an effort to keep warm. All of them – Frank, Wilf, Hassan and Michael – were thinking of hot baths and warm beds, and a few hours' sleep before they'd be back at the dock and waiting for another ship to come in. They shouldn't have been there at this hour, a little after midnight, but orders were orders, and besides, the boss had promised them extra pay for their efforts.

Even so, Frank, a burly man with a face full of burst capillaries and a tattoo of a naked woman on his right arm, had been complaining about it for much of the night. What was the point of a ship coming in to dock for one measly little crate? What was so bloody important about this crate in the first place?

Wilf was a little more complacent about being there. His wife was a dragon, and everyone knew it. No wonder he seemed more than happy to be standing on the edge of the dock at this ungodly hour, smoking Woodbines and talking about the football.

Hassan didn't say much, but then he never did. His English was still a long way from perfect, and when he swore it was usually in his native Somali. At twenty-six, he was closest in age to Michael, but tall and broad across the shoulders; quiet but handsome, with dark inscrutable eyes and a smile which, though it only made very rare appearances, lit up his face.

Michael was twenty-four, the youngest of the group. He was still referred to, by the others, as 'the lad' or 'the boy', being baby-faced and awkward; curly black hair and blue eyes, and a faraway dreamy look, as if his mind were often elsewhere. Though they had worked together the best part of eight years, he was still the target of their occasional jokes, both verbal and practical. His first few weeks in the docks had been full of pointless errands, like the time they'd sent him away to buy tartan paint, or the time they'd told him to pick up an order of sky hooks. Tonight the focus of their ridicule was Michael's date with Maggie Jenkins.

It was a date he hadn't even wanted to go on in the first place, having been coerced into it by his friends and workmates. He'd taken her to the Capitol Cinema on Queen

Street to watch a double bill of *Destination Moon* and *The Day the Earth Stood Still*. After the films, they had gone for a milkshake at Mario's on Caroline Street, where Michael had tried to do an impersonation of Richard Burton after Maggie told him how much she loved the actor's voice. Sadly it hadn't worked. She'd laughed and told him he sounded more like Paul Robeson with a cold.

'Didn't even get your hand in her blouse?' asked Frank, lighting up another fag and chuckling. The others laughed, even Hassan, who seemed to have an innate understanding of dirty jokes, if little else.

Michael blushed and shook his head. He didn't like it when Hassan laughed at him, but he was used to it by now.

'Look out, lads. Here she comes,' said Wilf, pointing out at the sea. There, coming through the shallow fog, was the grey hulk of the *Facklaträfat*, a Swedish cargo ship. It was only a small vessel, by the standard of some of the ships out there, but still, to Michael and the others, it seemed awfully big for just one crate.

Only a few hundred metres away, two men stood in front of the red-brick, gothic façade of the Pierhead Building, watching the progress of the *Facklaträfat* as it came in closer to the dock's edge. In physical appearance, they could hardly have been more different. The younger of the two, Valentine, was tall, gangling almost, with his hair Brylcreemed back above a high forehead. A deep scar made a canyon of the left side of his face, starting in one corner of

7

his mouth and travelling all the way up to the top of his ear. The older man, Cromwell, was short and stout, dressed in a trench coat and trilby. At a passing glance, he resembled the actor Orson Welles, all owl-like intensity and beady eyes.

'I still don't see why they couldn't wait for Nelson-Stanley to bring it back to London,' said Valentine, sniffing and rubbing his nose with the back of his hand.

Cromwell breathed heavily and looked up at his companion.

'Nelson-Stanley is in the Arctic for another three months. We couldn't leave it there that long. Not that close to the Russian territories. If the word from London is to be believed, those bloody Reds were already looking for it, although how they knew about it is anyone's guess. That bastard Philby, most likely, or one of his lot. Careless talk and all the rest of it.'

'Right you are, Mr Cromwell. Right you are.' Another sniff, another wipe of his nose. 'So how big is it?'

'How big?' said Cromwell, chuckling to himself. 'About the size of a football, so I'm told.'

'A football?' asked Valentine. 'A ship like that for something the size of a football?'

'Absolutely, Mr Valentine, absolutely. You know what they say. It's not the size that counts…'

Valentine smiled, but only on the right side of his face.

The crate was now only twenty feet off the edge of the dock, being lowered on a thick hemp rope. On the deck of the

Facklaträfat, one of the crew hollered to the crane operator, 'Sakta! Sakta!'

'Can you hear something?' said Frank.

'Yeah,' said Wilf. 'Someone talking in Swedish.'

Frank tutted. 'No, not that, you bloody idiot, something in the crate.'

Wilf cocked one ear towards the crate and frowned. 'No, Frank, I can't.'

'Listen. Listen a minute. Can you hear it?'

Michael followed Wilf's example and tilted his head so that one ear was aimed towards the crate. Frank was right. He *could* hear something. A strange, throbbing sound; familiar and yet at the same time unlike anything he had heard before.

'Yeah,' said Michael. 'I can hear it.'

'Me too,' said Hassan.

The crate was lower now, low enough for Hassan, who was taller than the others, to be able to touch it if he stood on his toes.

'Shaking,' he said. 'Like inside, there is something shaking.'

'Look, mate,' Frank called up to the man on the deck. 'What's inside this thing? What's that noise?'

'Jog förstår inte,' the man replied, shrugging.

'Bloody marvellous,' said Frank. 'They all speak double Dutch. Fat lot of use that is to us.'

'It's getting louder,' said Michael.

The crate lowered further, so that it was now only a few feet from the ground.

'I still can't hear anything,' said Wilf.

'No, well you wouldn't,' said Frank. 'You're bloody deaf from your wife nagging you all the time.'

The others laughed, and that was when the crate exploded with a blinding flash of light, and a force great enough to rock the ship towards its starboard.

Michael was blasted across the edge of the dock, one side of the crate hitting him face-on and carrying him ten metres until he fell to the ground with a heavy thump. A plume of intense heat erupted from the other side of the crate, sending a shard of wood through Frank's throat and a heavy iron nail into Wilf's chest. Hassan was blown from the dock into the side of the ship. He was unconscious when he landed, face down, in the water.

As fragments of burning wood and sawdust scorched into cinders rained down around the dock, another object came clattering down onto the cobbles: a metal sphere, no bigger than a football, and ruptured on one side. Had anyone been conscious to see it, they would have noticed a dull glow the colour of burning sulphur, and heard the sound of that throbbing as it grew quieter and quieter. The glow too died out, leaving just an empty metal shell.

It was mere moments before Cromwell and Valentine arrived on the scene. Cromwell was out of breath from running, but Valentine had barely broken a sweat. All about them were the bodies and the burning remains of the crate. On the deck of the ship, the Swedish crew were swearing and cursing, but neither man could understand them.

'A bomb?' suggested Valentine. 'The Russians?'

'I don't know,' said Cromwell, 'but we need to clear this up, and we need to speak to the crew of that ship.'

He stalked across the dock, toward the dull metal sphere that lay among the debris.

'They're dead,' he said, looking down at two of the bloodied corpses. 'Fewer witnesses.'

'Not all of them,' said Valentine.

Cromwell turned and saw Valentine lifting a heavy panel from on top of one of the bodies.

'This one's alive.'

Valentine hauled the panel clear of the unconscious young man and dropped it clattering to the ground. There was one word stencilled on its charred surface.

Torchwood.

ONE

Sundays were never Sundays at Torchwood, or at least not most of the time. Jack couldn't remember the last time he'd had a Sunday which felt how Sundays were supposed to feel. Wasn't Sunday the day when normal people ate slap-up breakfasts, took the dog for a walk and then spent the rest of the afternoon reading the papers?

But then, Captain Jack Harkness wasn't 'normal people' and, at Torchwood, Sundays were more likely to be spent doing work which the people of Cardiff, and indeed most of the six billion people on the planet, knew nothing about.

This Sunday was different. On this particular Sunday, Jack had even had a chance to clean the SUV. This was normally a task he'd delegate to Ianto, or anyone except himself but, if today was going to be one of the few boring Sundays he'd ever get to experience, he was going to spend it doing all the things normal people did.

The Rift was quiet. He'd had Toshiko spend much of the morning and afternoon checking all the equipment, making sure there wasn't a fault. As it turned out, there wasn't. Everything was working, the readings were accurate. The Rift, it seemed, was taking a day off. Having checked and double-checked everything, and satisfied herself that Rift activity was at a minimum, Toshiko was now looking into what she described as a 'low-resonance electromagnetic pulse' coming from the basement.

'Anything for me to worry about?' Jack asked, as he walked aimlessly past her workstation in the centre of the Hub.

'No, Jack. Probably nothing. I've picked it up once or twice before. I'm just trying to work out which one of our extraterrestrial *toys* it's coming from.'

Though her endless fascination with the occasionally dull minutiae of her job was sometimes baffling to Jack, he found it curiously reassuring, and so he left her to her work.

What he couldn't understand was why Gwen was still here. It was now a little after eight on a Sunday evening, nothing was happening, and yet she was still here, searching through files on her computer with the listless look of a teenager browsing through YouTube in the early hours of the morning.

'Now come on, Gwen,' said Jack, placing one hand on her shoulder, and putting on his best 'concerned parent' voice. 'The rest of us have excuses. We don't have lives. You do. What are you doing here?'

Gwen looked up at him with a scowl and a sigh that he wasn't quite expecting.

'Rhys,' she said. 'I… I just…'

'Arguing?'

'Yes.'

'Let me guess… About work?'

'No, actually.'

She huffed again and returned her gaze to the dull glow of her monitor.

'So what was it about?'

'Sofas.'

Jack took his hand off her shoulder and laughed through his nose, before realising that Gwen didn't find it funny.

'Sofas?' he said, trying hard to sound serious.

'Yes. Sofas. We went shopping yesterday afternoon to look for a sofa. I wanted this red one, he wanted this cream white leather thing that… God, it was just so tacky… Anyway…' She sighed. 'Sofas.'

'So there's a part of the world that still argues about sofas?' said Jack, still maintaining a veneer of sincerity. 'In a city which is home to one of the most active rifts in time and space this side of the Milky Way, you still argue about sofas?'

'What's that supposed to mean, Jack?'

'I mean… It's a sofa. Why don't you go home to Rhys, and… I don't know… get a takeaway and… do couply stuff. Aren't you meant to be enjoying love's young dream, what with that ring on your finger and all?'

'Jack, I'm working…'

'Gwen, there's no work to do. I've just cleaned the SUV, I've tidied most of our hard drives, I even changed a bulb in

15

my office earlier.'

'You cleaned the SUV?'

'Yes.'

Gwen laughed, putting one hand over her mouth.

'*You*… cleaned the SUV?'

'Yes. Is that so hard to believe?'

'I'm just imagining you like Jessica Simpson in that video…'

'Well, why don't you take your mental image, and *go*. Go on. That's an order. And where's Owen?'

'Down in the Vaults.'

'Tell him he can go too. It's the quietest night we've had in a year and you're all still here. You're insane. All of you.'

Gwen sighed and quickly shut down each application on her computer. She picked up her coat and, waving goodbye to Toshiko from across the Hub, made her way down to the Vaults.

Of all the parts of Torchwood, it was the Vaults that Gwen liked the least. She knew from past experience that it was possible for a place to physically soak up strong emotions. Somewhere in his safe, Jack had a machine capable of reading these things, but even without that device Gwen believed it was possible to sense the bad feelings left behind. When she was fifteen, she had gone on a history trip with her school to Germany where they had visited one of the old concentration camps. The atmosphere had been chilling; no sound of birdsong, no sound of anything, in fact, except their footsteps. It had seemed colder, too, the minute they had passed through the gates.

Though the scale and context were quite different the Vaults in Torchwood reminded her of that feeling; the sudden plunge of temperature, and a strange melancholy which she couldn't quite place. It was as if she felt sad for all the people and creatures who had ended up in those cells; scared, and angry, lost and alone.

It made it all the more mysterious that Owen should want to spend the whole afternoon and evening down there, sat on a stool, peering through the glass of one of the cells at Janet.

Janet was a Weevil; that is, an occasionally carnivorous life form that had slipped through the Rift and into Cardiff's sewers. Occasionally, one or more of the Weevils would come up to the surface, and sometimes they developed a taste for something other than the effluent diet on which they usually survived.

'Hey, Owen,' said Gwen as she stepped down into the dark and narrow corridor that ran alongside the cells. 'What you up to?'

'I'm writing a musical about my experiences with Torchwood,' said Owen. 'I'm gonna call it "Weevil Rock You".'

'Oh, Owen, that's not funny,' said Gwen, laughing. 'What are you really up to?'

'I'm keeping an eye on Janet,' he said. 'Something's wrong with her.'

'Her?'

'Her. It. Whatever.'

'So what's wrong?'

17

Gwen looked into the cell. Janet was stood in the corner, shoulders hunched, facing the wall. Every so often, it would make a low, gurgling sound, and paw at the damp brick wall with one hand.

'That,' said Owen. 'She keeps doing that. Every twenty-six minutes. Then she'll sit down, and maybe try and sleep or something, and then bam – twenty-six minutes later, she's back up.'

'Exactly twenty-six minutes?'

'Yeah. For the last four hours.'

Gwen shook her head and sighed.

'Jack's right,' she said. 'We're all insane. It's a Sunday night, and you're here watching the resident Weevil, Tosh is upstairs doing… I don't know… Tosh things…'

'Ianto?'

'I don't know. I haven't seen Ianto.'

Ianto Jones was at his station behind the run-down Tourist Information Centre that served as a front to the clandestine goings-on in Torchwood. His bare feet were on his desk, his tie slumped like a crestfallen snake next to an open pizza box, the top two buttons of his shirt undone.

'Taking it easy, I see?' said Jack, stepping out through the security door that led into the Hub itself. 'Well, at least someone has the right idea. Whatcha doing there, Sport?'

'"Sport"?' said Ianto. 'Not sure I like "Sport" as a term of endearment. "Sexy" is good, if unimaginative. "Pumpkin" is a bit much, but "Sport"? No. You'll have to think of another one.'

'OK, Tiger Pants. Whatcha doing?'

Ianto laughed.

'I…' he said, pausing to swallow a mouthful of pizza, 'am having a James Bondathon.'

'A what?'

'A James Bondathon. I'm watching my favourite James Bond films, in chronological order.'

'You're a Bond fan?'

'Oh yes. He's the archetypal male fantasy, isn't he? The man all women want to have, and all men want to be.'

'Are you sure it's not the other way around?'

Ianto raised an eyebrow and took another bite of his pizza.

'Hey,' said Jack. 'I'm sending everyone home. There's nothing happening here. The Rift is still giving out minimal readings. Gwen's going home, Owen's going home, and I think Tosh is almost done.'

'The place to ourselves?'

'Well…' said Jack, grinning.

'So long as it's not going to interrupt my James Bondathon. I've only just started watching *Goldfinger*, and I haven't even reached the bit where Shirley Eaton gets painted gold yet.'

'OK… Well, I'll just say goodbye to Owen and Gwen, and tell Tosh to wrap up, and then—'

Jack didn't have a chance to finish his sentence. Even if he had, it was doubtful Ianto could have heard him, as the air was pierced by the shrill sound of the alarm.

'What is it?' Ianto asked, his fingers in his ears. 'Fire?'

'Jack…' It was Toshiko, speaking over the comms. 'We've got an intruder.'

Gwen and Owen were leaving Janet and the holding cells when the alarm rang out and they heard Toshiko's voice.

'Owen, Gwen, I need you up here immediately. We have an intruder. Hurry!'

Owen bolted out through the door and Gwen followed. Together, they ran through the dark, dank corridors of Torchwood until they came out into the Hub. Toshiko was standing at her workstation, pale and stunned.

'What is it?' asked Owen. 'Who's here?'

'There's somebody in the basement,' said Toshiko. 'I was monitoring the pulse, and then… I checked one of the cameras, and there's a man down there. Where's Jack?'

On cue, Jack entered the Hub with Ianto. Seeing Ianto with bare feet and a dishevelled shirt, Owen turned to Gwen and raised an eyebrow, but it did nothing to calm her nerves. How could somebody have got into the basement? More importantly, who or *what* was in there?

As Toshiko turned off the alarm, Jack ran across the Hub to her workstation and looked down at the monitor.

'It looks like a man,' he said. 'It looks human, at least. Tosh… How the hell did he get in there?'

'I don't know, Jack. I was tracing the pulse, and I narrowed it down to Basement D-4. There was nothing there, and then… and then the image turned to static, and when the picture came back he was there. I've scanned the whole room; he's definitely human.'

The image on the screen showed the basement, filmed from an upper corner. In the dim light, Jack could just about see a man, sat on the ground and hugging his knees.

'And the pulse,' said Toshiko. 'It was temporal before, coming and going, but now it's constant. I thought it might be an electromagnetic wave, like radiation, but I'm not sure. It's not like any kind of radiation I've seen before.'

'OK,' said Jack. 'I need to go down there.'

'I'm coming, too,' said Owen.

'No you're not,' said Jack. 'We could have the human equivalent of Chernobyl sitting in our basement if Tosh's readings are correct. I need to go down alone. I need a Geiger counter.'

Toshiko ran to her workstation and opened a drawer, rifling through her collection of screwdrivers, soldering irons, and pliers.

'Here,' she said eventually. 'It's charged.'

Jack took the counter from her and headed out of the Hub. As he ran past, Ianto tried to say something, but couldn't. It was no use; none of them could stop him at a time like this. It was times like this that reminded them exactly whose organisation this was. They might be a team, and a team that had coped without him, but he was still the one in charge.

'I was so bored,' said Gwen. 'I actually thought at one point, "Please let something interesting happen, I'm so bored".' She shook her head, and turned to Owen. 'Remind me never, ever to think that again. I was so much happier when I was bored.'

'Liar,' said Owen.

Jack stepped down towards Basement D-4. It was the first time he'd been there in a very long time. Even in a building this sealed off from the outside world, there was still a lot of dust. Dust, and spiders' webs, and all the evidence, if it were needed, that life finds a way of getting into even the most apparently sterile environments. It unnerved Jack a little to think, if spiders could get in, what else might be able to get out.

Worse still, the Geiger counter was picking up next to nothing. If the electromagnetic waves weren't conventional radiation, that left only one possibility as far as he was concerned, and he didn't want to consider what that meant. As he neared the entrance to D-4, a metre-and-a-half-thick steel door, he brushed those thoughts away as easily as he had the spiders' webs. Someone was on the other side of the door. Someone that didn't belong there. He had to stay focused on that. Someone had got in through a room that hadn't been opened in thirty years or more. Someone was in there, and alive, in a place where the oxygen itself was stale and about as old as his staff.

Jack punched a code into a panel at the side of the door, and waited four seconds before he heard the locks clank open inside. The door opened, and it sounded as if the room itself were breathing in. A gust of cool, fresh air (or as fresh as the air in Torchwood could be) swept in, and that old, dry, dusty air came out. Jack had, in his time, been in far too many crypts and sepulchres, of many different kinds, on many different worlds, and that was exactly what this felt like. It felt dead.

'Hello…' said Jack, taking his revolver from its holster and holding it at his side. 'Hello… Can you hear me?'

His voice echoed around inside the room, but no reply came.

'OK… I'm going to come in now. But I warn you – I'm armed.'

As he stepped into the room, he saw the same figure that he had seen on Toshiko's monitor, a man hunched over on the floor, still holding his knees to his chest.

'Hello?' said Jack.

There was something about the man's clothes that was familiar to him. They didn't belong in Cardiff in 2008, that was for sure. He'd seen clothes like that many years before, the kind of utility clothes that everyone had after the war; drab and grey and lacking in any kind of ostentation.

'Are you OK?' said Jack. 'I'm not going to hurt you.'

He thought he could hear sobbing.

The man on the floor looked up with eyes bloodshot from tears and an expression of absolute terror, and Jack gasped. He dropped his gun to the ground, and fell back against the wall of the vault.

'Michael…' he said.

TWO

'Jack?'

He'd been sitting alone in his office for ten minutes, while Owen and Gwen were taking Michael from Basement D-4 to the Boardroom; ten minutes in which he had done nothing but think, and yet those thoughts were still so clouded. How could he have allowed himself to be blindsided like this? How could he not have known this was going to happen?

Decades spent knowing the future had, he supposed, left him with a kind of complacency; a resignation to the future and the concept of destiny. There was no point in fighting the future, or destiny, and so very little surprised him these days. Why had this hit him so hard?

'Jack?'

He looked over at the door. Gwen was standing in the entrance to his office, leaning against the doorframe, smiling softly.

'You OK, Jack?'

He shook off his mood, at least on the outside, and smiled back.

'Yeah. I'm fine,' he said. 'I'm just glad our guest doesn't have six arms and a penchant for human flesh.'

Gwen laughed.

'You sure you're OK? I was watching the monitor, when you were down there. You looked like you'd seen a ghost.'

'Yeah.' He paused, and then, with greater certainty, said 'Yeah. I'm fine. How is he?'

'Michael?'

Jack took a deep breath. 'Yeah. Michael.'

'He's fine. A little shaken up. A little disorientated. But he's OK now. Owen's giving him his usual, sensitive bedside manner. You know how Owen is.'

'By sensitive bedside manner I take it you mean the third degree?'

'Something like that.' Gwen smiled, but the smile faded quickly. 'We've established that his name is Michael Bellini and that he's twenty-four. He said you knew his name.'

'What's that?'

'Michael. He said you knew his name. He said you called him "Michael".'

'He must have been confused.'

'Are you sure?' asked Gwen.

'Yes.'

'Oh. Because… I thought I recognised him. I don't know where from, but it's like déjà vu or something. Or like when you see somebody you recognise off the telly.'

'I don't know him.'

26

Gwen nodded, biting her lip. What was Jack hiding? He'd been so secretive about so many things, and every time it put her on edge. She trusted him, they *all* trusted him, but sometimes it was as if they didn't know him at all.

'So are you coming down?' she asked.

Jack shook his head. 'No,' he said. 'Not yet. I've got a few things need doing here. You go on down. I'll join you as soon as I'm finished.'

Gwen left Jack's office and walked down to the Boardroom. Michael was sat in a chair at one end of the conference table, while Owen took his blood pressure. Ianto and Toshiko stood in the far corners of the room.

As Gwen entered the Boardroom, Michael looked at her, wide-eyed and lost, and then at the others.

'Here, Gwen…' said Owen, 'listen to this.' He turned to Michael. 'Who's the Prime Minister of Great Britain?'

'W-Winston Churchill,' said Michael, his voice barely louder than a whisper.

'OK… And who's at number one in the charts?'

'Frankie Lane.'

Owen turned to Gwen, his arms open as if he were the ringmaster of a circus presenting the next act.

'Owen, quit it,' said Gwen. She looked at Michael. The young man looked so scared, it didn't seem fair turning him into a freak show.

'He's from 1953,' said Owen. 'Or, to be exact, November the twentieth 1953. Churchill is Prime Minister, and Frankie Lane is at number one with… Hang on. Michael, what was that song called?'

'"Answer Me",' Michael replied, timidly.

'Owen, I said quit it. This isn't some kind of game show.' Gwen turned to Michael. 'Do you know how you got here?'

Michael shook his head.

'Do you remember where you're from?'

Michael nodded. 'Cardiff,' he said. 'Butetown. I live on Fitzhamon Terrace. Where am I?'

Gwen looked at the others. 'You didn't tell him?'

The others shrugged.

Gwen sighed and leaned back against the wall. She looked to the ceiling for an easy way to say this. How could you tell someone they were so far away from home? She'd sometimes felt as lost and as scared as he did now, especially in the early days. What could she say to him?

'You're still in Cardiff,' she said at last. 'But it's not 1953. That was more than fifty years ago.'

Michael's eyes filled with tears once more, and he let out a shuddering, helpless sob.

'But… But that means I'm almost eighty…'

'No,' said Gwen, smiling gently, trying to put him at ease. 'You're not eighty. You're still you. You're just here.'

'But the future?' Michael shook his head. 'How can I be here? How can any of this be happening?'

'Wait,' said Gwen, turning to Toshiko. '1953? We've had visitors from 1953 before. Do you think this could be connected to that?'

Owen looked up suddenly, his expression a curious mixture of shock and hope.

'I don't think so,' said Toshiko. 'They flew through the Rift in the *Sky Gypsy*. It wasn't the Rift that brought Michael here. It's clearly got something to do with the pulse that I was picking up earlier. The curious thing is, since we brought Michael here, I'm now picking up two definable sources for it.'

'Two?'

Toshiko nodded. 'Yes. Michael and Basement D-4.'

'What does all this mean?' said Michael, growing angrier. 'You're all talking rubbish. None of this makes sense. It's a nightmare, isn't it? It's a bad dream? It's got to be a bad dream. I've been watching too many of those stupid bloody films at the pictures. All those films about flying saucers and spaceships…'

'You're not dreaming,' said Gwen. 'What's the last thing you remember, before you were here?'

Michael looked down at the ground, and his shoulders shook with another barely suppressed sob.

It was like stepping off the roller-coaster at first, that feeling of nausea, and of senses overloaded. It took a few seconds for the white noise and for the light behind his eyelids to go away, and for him to realise that he was on his hands and knees, and that the ground beneath him was hard, and cold, and wet.

Then there was the noise.

He couldn't say that he had never heard it before, because he had, but many years ago. Like thunder, only it was worse than thunder. It was louder than thunder as if somebody was slamming a colossal door, and every time the door slammed the ground beneath him shook.

Above that slamming sound there was the drone, that unmistakable drone, like a million angry hornets. The Heinkel bombers. After five months, they had all learnt the difference between the sounds of the British and German planes.

Michael got to his feet and looked around. He was in the lane, *his* lane, at the end of Neville Street. Years ago, when he was a child, he had played in this lane, flicking pennies against the wall and kicking a ball about with Tommo and Mogs. Only, he suddenly realised, it wasn't years ago. Those games had happened at the same time that German bombers swarmed overhead and the howl of air-raid sirens would send people running for shelter.

The bombers hadn't been aiming for the houses, of course, they were going for the train tracks and the depot. It just happened that the houses were built around both.

He stepped out into Neville Street and saw the night sky lit up like Hell. He remembered somebody telling him that the only reason the bombers got this far was that the anti-aircraft guns on Ely Racecourse had malfunctioned, only that wasn't many years ago. It was now.

It was 2 January 1941, and Michael Bellini was walking down the street where he had grown up as a child, a street he hadn't revisited in more than a decade. There, on both sides of the street, were houses that neither he, nor anyone else for that matter, had seen in all those years, and yet they were still standing. There, running out of their front door, were Mr and Mrs Davies, with Mrs Davies holding her pet Yorkshire terrier under her arm. There, in the middle of the street, was Mr Harris, the ARP warden, self-important in his tin helmet, barking orders at them to get to shelter, and quickly.

Michael was wondering whether anyone could see him, when his question was answered by Mr Harris.

'Oi, you… Lad! Get inside, quick. This isn't a walk along the bloody promenade. It's an air raid!'

He had heard him say those words before; it wasn't déjà vu. Michael had heard Mr Harris say those exact words, with that exact voice. Looking further down the street, past Mr Harris, he saw three figures outside the open door of number 26; a boy no older than eleven, an older girl, and a woman, her hair still in curlers.

Michael thought for a moment that his heart might stop, or that he would finally, thankfully wake up, but he didn't. Running from their house and out into Neville Street, he saw his mother, his sister Maria, and himself.

Mr Harris did an about-turn, and starting yelling at the three of them and, though Michael couldn't hear what he was saying over the drone of the planes and the slam and the roar of the explosions, he could remember. Mr Harris was asking them where they were going, and Michael's mother was telling him that they were going to her sister's house on Clare Road, because they had an Anderson shelter there. Mr Harris told them to hurry up while they were at it, and so they started running.

Michael knew what happened next.

They were halfway down Neville Street when Michael's mother stopped in her tracks. She had told him and his sister to carry on running until they reached Aunty Megan's, and then she had run back to the house. Maybe she had forgotten something.

As he watched himself and his sister running to the end of the street, Michael suddenly realised that this was his chance. Maybe this was why he was here. Maybe this time it could be different. He started running towards the house he had grown up in, heedless of the sound of bombs and the drone of the planes. He ran towards it knowing what was going to happen, and he cried out: 'Mum!'

The bomb didn't hit their house directly; it landed somewhere in the gardens behind their street. Michael and his sister had been on Clare Road at the time, crying and scared, not knowing what had happened.

Facing it for the first time, Michael saw the explosion almost a split second before he could hear it; a blinding flash of white light and then a fireball that erupted upwards and outwards, destroying a whole row of houses as if they were made of nothing more than sand and matchsticks.

The sound and the shockwave knocked him off his feet, and suddenly everything was dark, and all he could hear was the roar of the fire and the sound of bricks, and wood, and glass raining down upon the cold, damp street.

He struggled to his feet, and saw the gaping crater filled with fire where their house had been, the neighbouring houses now hollowed out like dead teeth, the street itself shoulder-deep in debris.

He wiped the tears now streaming from his eyes away from his face and saw that they had been turned to ink by soot and ash. He put one hand to his chest and felt a sliver of wood sticking out of his shirt. Just touching it sent a hot bolt of pain through his chest.

'The Traveller…'

Somebody was calling him, only they weren't *calling* him. They weren't even raising their voice. It was like a whisper that he could somehow hear over the din of the fire and the bombers and the sound of people screaming.

'The Traveller…'

He turned and saw a man walking through the flames. A man dressed smartly in a black suit and bowler hat, and carrying an umbrella.

That was when he blacked out.

THREE

'I couldn't stop it from happening,' Michael said, his head in his hands. 'I thought maybe I could, but it still happened. Everything happens.'

Gwen felt herself shudder, and the hairs on the back of her neck stood to attention, though she still couldn't quite fathom why. Owen had left the Boardroom, saying he had to 'go check something', so it was just three of them, now, with Michael.

Gwen didn't want to believe a word he had said; she wanted to think it was some elaborate fantasy, and a younger, less experienced Gwen might have believed that, but she knew better. She liked to think she was a good judge of honesty, that she knew when people were lying; it came with the job. She knew Michael was telling the truth.

'OK,' she said. 'Then you came here? After the explosion? That's when you woke up here?'

'No… I don't know,' said Michael. 'I don't think so.'

'And what about before…' Gwen paused. She had to

word this carefully. 'Before 1941. Where were you before you found yourself in 1941? What happened in 1953?'

He hadn't yet dared to open his eyes. At first, the voices were little more than a vague mumbling that seemed to echo, as if they were speaking inside a cavern or a cathedral, but eventually he could hear and recognise words.

He heard a man's voice.

'Well, Margaret, quite frankly if he's the one playing hard to get I'd drop him like a hot brick. Men like that aren't worth it.'

'I know.' A woman's voice, now. 'But I was really looking forward to the dance. He's a pig.'

'He's worse than a pig, Margaret, he's a swine. The silly bugger. There's half the men in this hospital would give their right arm to go on a date with a girl like you.'

'Half the men?'

'Well, half the men who aren't acquainted with musical theatre, if you know what I mean… But you know what I mean.'

Both voices laughed, but stopped abruptly when Michael groaned. He was aware of pain. Pain across his chest, in his head, his neck – in fact, he couldn't find a part of his body that didn't hurt. On top of that, he was dehydrated. His tongue felt like sandpaper on the roof of his mouth, and his lips tasted of blood.

'Oh, somebody's awake,' said the male voice. 'Margaret, you go and get Dr Hutchins and I'll demonstrate my bedside manner.'

'I bet you will.'

The curtain opened and, when Michael first opened his eyes, it was as if he were stood before a floodlight. There was a white flash of light, something which caused his heart to pick up pace, and then shapes and forms slowly became visible until finally he was looking up at a male nurse.

'Good morning, sunshine… Now, can you just tell me your name?'

Michael mouthed his name but no sound came out. His throat was still dry and he was suddenly aware of something tickling at the back of his throat. The nurse held up three fingers on his left hand.

'How many fingers am I holding up?'

'Th… three…' Michael whispered.

'Do you know where you are?'

He nodded.

'Can you remember what happened?'

He shook his head. What had happened? Why was he in a hospital?

'OK. Don't move. Just stay there… That's it… Don't want to go doing yourself an injury. Now, what's the name of the Prime Minister?'

'Winston Churchill.' Michael croaked.

The nurse beamed down at him.

'That's right,' he said. 'OK, Michael, I'm Nurse Collins. Nurse Gait has just gone to fetch Dr Hutchins. She won't be a moment.'

Dr Hutchins was a balding man with pince-nez glasses and a bow tie, and a shock of white hair at the back of his head. At the top of his forehead there was an indented yellow scar that Michael thought might have been an injury from the war; the first one, that is. When he spoke, it was in the curt fashion of somebody who had served in the military, so it wasn't beyond speculation. Even so there was something kindly and reassuring about him, something that put Michael at ease.

'You're in the Royal Infirmary, Michael. You've been here for four days now, in body, if not in spirit. Do you remember the accident?'

Michael shook his head.

'What accident?' he asked.

'You were working a late shift, at the docks. There was an explosion. Something to do with paraffin so your employer told us.'

An explosion. He could remember an explosion, or at least he thought he could. His mind flooded with images of another time in his life when there had been fire and pain, but it wasn't that. This was different.

'Fortunately your injuries do not appear to be as severe as we first feared. A few bumps and scratches, and you cracked a rib, but nothing broken. Nothing we can't mend.'

There was a crate. He could remember the crate, and the ship. He had been there with Frank, and Wilf, and Hassan.

'Hassan…' he said, 'and the others. What about the others?'

Dr Hutchins took off his glasses and bit his lower lip.

'I'm sorry, Michael,' he said. 'I don't know how to tell you this, but they weren't as lucky as you.'

Standing, Dr Hutchins turned to Nurse Collins.

'Are there any family we need to notify?'

'Yes,' said Nurse Collins. 'His sister. She lives in Butetown. She was here yesterday.'

Dr Hutchins nodded, and then looked back down at Michael. He smiled. It was a smile Michael supposed he gave all his patients, especially, perhaps, the ones he felt sorry for. As he left the ward, Nurses Collins and Gait followed, and Michael was alone.

His sister came to see him later that afternoon. Her eyes were bloodshot, and she wasn't wearing any make-up. He couldn't remember the last time he'd seen her without make-up. Perhaps when their father had died.

'I was so worried,' she said, squeezing his hand so hard it almost hurt. 'When they told me, about Frank, and Wilf, and the other boy—'

'Hassan,' said Michael, tearfully.

'Oh God,' said his sister. 'I didn't want to lose you. I mean, I've got Rhodri, and the baby, but you… You're my brother.'

She kissed him on the forehead before leaving, and told him there would be a roast dinner waiting for him when he got home. It made him happy to see her smiling when she left.

He slept badly that night. The old man in the bed opposite spent much of the night wailing, crying out for the nurses and his 'Mam', even though he couldn't have been any younger than eighty. Michael could do little more than look out through his window at the night sky and the waning moon, and think about nothing else but the crate and the explosion.

He could remember everything now; the Swedish ship appearing through the fog, the noise inside the crate, and then the blast. Something had happened during the explosion, something he couldn't describe. To him it hadn't sounded like an explosion. He had heard bombs as a child, and it hadn't sounded like that. It had sounded like a bass drum, or perhaps the single ringing of an enormous bell, somewhere inside of him. His whole body had tingled as if he were being pricked by hundreds of thousands of microscopic pins and, though his eyes were closed, he could still see that brilliant white light, like a billion suns; a light that seemed to pass through him.

In the morning he was woken by Nurse Collins, who removed the gastric tube from his nose, which caused him to gag, and brought him a cup of tea and a slice of half-burnt toast. The old man in the bed opposite was now sleeping like a baby, worn out, presumably, by a night of anguished crying.

It was mid-morning when the visitors arrived.

Two men, both dressed in suits. One was in his early thirties, Michael guessed; the other looked a little older. The younger, taller man had a dramatic scar on the left side of his face and a hang-dog expression. The older and shorter man had large, dark eyes and heavy eyebrows. Sitting in a chair beside the bed, it was the older man who spoke first.

'Good morning, Mr Bellini. I trust you're feeling well?'

Michael nodded and asked them who they were.

'My name is Mr Cromwell, and this is Mr Valentine. We work for the Union. We're just here to ask you a few questions.'

Michael nodded again, but said nothing.

'Do you remember anything about the explosion on Thursday night?'

Michael thought for a moment. How should he answer their question? Something about this didn't feel right. They didn't look like anyone from the Union. They looked like policemen.

'No,' he said at last. 'Not much. Nothing, really.'

Cromwell looked up at Valentine, and then turned back to Michael. 'I see. We're still investigating the cause of the explosion. It's possible there may have been an issue with certain materials that were in the vicinity.'

And that line. It didn't sound right. It was clumsy, as if Cromwell was stalling, or making it up as he went along.

'Other than your injuries have you noticed any other… problems… at all?' asked Cromwell.

Michael shook his head.

'Any feelings of nausea? Headaches? Strange dreams?'

Why would somebody from the Union need to know anything about headaches or strange dreams? Michael looked out into the corridor, hoping to catch the attention of one of the nurses. If he could only pretend to be in more pain, they might come in and tell Cromwell and Valentine to give him a little peace.

'Have you experienced anything… unusual?' Cromwell asked.

41

'No,' said Michael. 'No… I… nothing like that, no.'

'I see. Well, we may need to ask you a few more questions when you're feeling a little bit better. You aren't planning on leaving Cardiff any time soon, are you?'

Michael shook his head.

'Good. Good. Well, I think we're done for now. We'll speak to you again, Mr Bellini. Get well soon.'

Cromwell stood, and both he and Valentine gave Cheshire cat grins that didn't sit comfortably on their faces, particularly Valentine's, before they walked out of the ward.

Michael was released from the hospital the following day. There was nobody to meet him at the door. His sister was working at the cigarette factory and his brother-in-law, Rhodri, was at the docks. Though his legs still ached, he walked all the way back to Butetown in the plain, drab and ill-fitting clothes that the hospital had given him.

By the time he reached the narrow and canyon-like streets of Butetown that surrounded Tiger Bay, it was late afternoon, and already he could hear piano music spilling out of the pubs. He heard the raucous laughter of the Irishmen playing cards, and the incomprehensible chattering of the Chinese women in the laundries. Children played in the streets where sailors sauntered toward brothels, while the occasional policeman turned a blind eye to anything that wasn't threatening to turn into a brawl.

These sights were familiar to him by now, of course. He'd lived in the shadowy and smoke-filled confines of

Butetown since his mother died. Their father had brought them down here to be closer to his work at the docks, when he was still working. Soon enough, of course, he'd lost his job; a short while after, he started drinking. They'd lived together, his father, his sister and Michael, in the downstairs of a terraced house, beneath a first-generation Italian family that argued and fought at all hours.

Michael knew Butetown like the back of his hand and yet, walking back into it that afternoon, it felt as if something had changed. The buildings looked different, somehow, as if they'd been remade from a different stone. Everything seemed more real.

The tiny house on Fitzhamon Terrace that he shared with his sister's family embraced him with the smell of a leg of lamb roasting slowly in the oven. He sat alone in the kitchen, drinking tea and smoking cigarettes until his sister came home, carrying his baby nephew over the threshold.

'Oh, you're home!' she said excitedly. 'Let me just put Robert in his cot. Food won't be long, and Rhodri's home soon.'

Rhodri was a little older than Michael and his sister, a surly and sardonic man who Michael had always found strangely intimidating. He'd never been sure what Maria saw in him, but she had always been quick to point out that without Rhodri they'd be homeless. Once he'd finished his shift at the docks, and spent the best part of half an hour soaking in the bath in the lean-to, the family sat around the table, with baby Robert in his high chair, playing with a plastic rattle and a teething ring.

Rhodri was helping himself to roast potatoes when he finally spoke. 'Funny thing, that explosion,' he said, in his usual, gruff tone.

'What do you mean, "funny"?' said Michael, barely able to mask his resentment.

'Well, they've closed off the whole dock, and that ship's still there. There were people all over it this morning. No crew. Just people, and jeeps. Like army jeeps. Funny thing. They reckon it was a bomb.'

Michael pretended not to listen, spooning carrots and then peas onto his plate before reaching across the table for the gravy boat.

'No police, mind,' said Rhodri, 'which is the *really* funny thing. You'd have thought, big explosion like that, they'd have had the police involved.'

When Michael looked up from his plate, he saw Rhodri, staring at him with an expression that bordered on amusement. It was too much to hope that his brother-in-law might realise quite how much this had all meant to him; seeing his friends killed like that. Frank and Wilf. Hassan.

When the meal was over, Michael went to his room, barely saying another word to either Maria or Rhodri, and only managing to muster a moment's baby talk with his nephew. Lying back on his bed, he turned on the radio. They were playing that song again, that Frankie Lane song they were playing all the time. He'd thought it was the most romantic song he'd ever heard before; before all this. Now just listening to it was painful. Why did they have to keep playing it?

He put his shoes back on and left the house in a flurry. His sister ran to the front door, and called after him, 'Michael! Where are you going?'

'Out,' he called back, sullenly. 'I won't be late.'

The Ship and Pilot was a typical Butetown pub, filled with the usual Butetown patrons: a mixture of dockers, sailors and waifs and strays from every corner of the globe. Gruff old men with stories to tell sat quietly nursing their pints and playing dominos while Michael's peers took part in all the rituals of youth, knocking back their pints of Brains bitter, telling jokes, or challenging anyone within earshot to an arm wrestle.

People were looking at him strangely, he could sense that much. They must have heard about what had happened, but nobody said anything. It was just the way they looked at him.

In the far corner of the pub, they were setting up the stage for Shirley, the resident singer, and her band, but the noisy chatter of the pub carried on unabated.

'What happened?'

Michael looked up. It was Frank's son, Pete. He was a little older than Michael, but built like his father, a natural born scrapper with forearms like Popeye's. The curious thing was, he didn't really look angry, and Pete almost always looked angry, like he was on the lookout for a fight. Now he just looked sad, like something inside of him had been crushed out of existence. Michael said nothing.

'What happened?' Pete asked again. 'You were there with him when it happened. *What* happened?'

'I don't know,' said Michael. 'I can't remember.'

'You can't remember? I . . .' Pete looked up into one corner of the room, breathed in deep, and closed his eyes.

'Honestly, Pete,' said Michael, 'I can't remember anything. There was an explosion, and then I woke up in hospital. That's all I can remember.'

'But what were you doing there at that time of night?'

'I don't know,' said Michael. 'I don't know.'

The rest of the pub had fallen quiet now, as Shirley took to the stage and opened her set with 'Stormy Weather'. Pete stared down at Michael with an intensity that scared him, signs of the Pete he knew, the angry, violent Pete, returning. Michael stood, leaving his pint glass half-full.

'I'm sorry, Pete,' he said, walking out of the pub. 'Really. I'm so sorry.'

He was halfway up the narrow, Victorian gully of West Bute Street, at the corner of the Coal Exchange, when he saw them.

Cromwell and Valentine.

They were standing in the shadows, but he could see them both. It was as if they weren't even trying to hide. He knew then for certain that they weren't from the Union.

He carried on walking, gathering pace, and somewhere behind him he could hear the sound of two men running, then sounds of a car engine grumbling into life, its wheels spinning against wet cobbles.

Michael started to run.

He was caught in the headlights, but he didn't dare look back. Why were they chasing him?

It was then that he felt it; a strange sensation starting in his feet and then creeping up his body until it reached his scalp, almost like static electric shocks. The streets around him were lit up with a brilliant light, impossible at this time of night, and everything was silent. He turned to face the oncoming car and saw that it had stopped in the middle of the street, its headlamps still glaring. Behind it, Cromwell and Valentine too had frozen on the spot, feet off the ground, as if suspended there on invisible strings. It was as if the world itself had stopped turning, just for him.

Then there was the pain. A terrible pain that surged through him, throbbing and pounding him into submission until he fell to the ground, his eyes clenched shut in agony. A few seconds passed, and with it a feeling of nausea, and then he realised that he was on his hands and knees, that the ground beneath him was hard, and cold, and wet, and that he could hear the sound of bombs.

'Cromwell and Valentine?' said Gwen. 'The names of the two men were Cromwell and Valentine?'

Michael nodded.

'And all this happened in *November* 1953?'

'Yes,' said Michael.

Gwen turned to Toshiko. 'Where's Owen?'

'He's down in the Autopsy Room. He said he had to check something.'

'OK,' said Gwen, 'can you go get him? We need to start looking into this.'

'What about Jack?' asked Toshiko.

'He's in his office. Something's wrong with him. I just don't know what.'

Gwen looked at Ianto, hoping he might have an answer, but he looked as puzzled as she was.

'Ianto,' she said. 'Can you carry out a search on the names Cromwell and Valentine? Can't be many people in Cardiff called Valentine in 1953.'

Ianto nodded stoically and left the Boardroom, and Toshiko followed.

Gwen turned to Michael. 'You rest a while,' she said. 'We're going to…' Her voice trailed off.

'Going to what?' Michael asked.

'I don't know,' said Gwen. 'We're going to help you.'

Michael looked away from her, forlorn. He didn't seem convinced by her reassurance.

'I mean it,' she said. 'It's what we do.' And then, smiling, 'No mystery too big, no puzzle too… erm… puzzling.'

Michael smiled, for the first time since she'd seen him, and Gwen felt something, a flicker of recognition, and an uneasy sense that this was going to be a long night.

FOUR

Owen Harper opened his eyes and saw a ceiling he didn't recognise. Not that he was an expert on ceilings, of course, but he knew his own ceiling when he saw it, and this wasn't his ceiling.

Next up was the awareness that his mouth was dry. No, not just dry… His mouth was desiccated. And then there was the headache. It felt like somebody had put his head in a vice and was still cranking it up. It felt like his head was going to explode.

But first was the matter of the ceiling and the hard floor beneath him. Reaching out with his fingertips, he felt the bristly surface of a carpet and, reaching further, his fingers delved into the dusty mess of an overflowing ashtray. He recoiled in disgust, and his hand brushed against the side of a can, tipping it over on its side. He heard the *glug-glug-fizz* of beer pouring from the can and soaking into the carpet. This wasn't a bed, and this wasn't a bedroom.

Through his one open eye, he saw a television in one

corner of the room, and on the wall several posters of Johnny Depp.

If it wasn't his ceiling, then it wasn't his living room, and if it wasn't his living room, then whose living room was it?

The answer came in a voice from the nearest doorway.

'Oh, you're awake. Did you fall off the sofa or something?'

He sat up straight, and that was when his head really began to throb; a dull pulsating agony that started in his temples and reached all the way in behind his eyes. The medic in him lectured him on the dehydrating effects of alcohol, how it leached moisture from the brain, causing it to shrink, pulling on all the microscopic fibres linking it to the skull and resulting in a headache. The human in him was simply practising the art of suffering.

In the doorway stood a goth girl in pyjamas. The pyjamas weren't particularly goth; pink with pictures of Hello Kitty. She was a goth girl only from the neck up, a shock of black hair and slightly smudged mascara left over from the night before.

His heart sank. Had they…?

'Where am I?' he asked.

'Our living room, silly,' replied the goth girl, giggling.

'And… where is your living room?' asked Owen.

'In our house. In Cathays,' said the goth girl. 'Near the uni.'

Owen sat fully upright and, with weak arms, hoisted himself onto the sofa. He rested his head in both hands and let out a long, traumatised groan.

'Hung over?' asked the goth girl.

'A little,' said Owen. 'What happened last night?'

The goth girl laughed again. 'You don't remember?'

Owen shook his head. Even *that* hurt.

'Your friend's upstairs,' she said, 'with my housemate, Kirsty. I'm amazed they didn't keep you awake. They were a bit, um, *noisy*. Mind you, you just kind of passed out.'

His friend? Oh, that was right. A little bit of memory came back to him now; a mere shard of recollection. Lloyd was upstairs. With Kirsty, whoever Kirsty was.

Owen looked at the goth girl, wincing at the question he was about to ask. 'And did anything... I mean...'

The goth girl raised one eyebrow, and shook her head. 'You're fully dressed,' she said. 'Or hadn't you noticed?'

He looked down at himself, and realised he was indeed still wearing all the clothes he'd worn the night before. He was dismayed to see a gory dash of chilli sauce down the front of his shirt. At least he'd remembered to take his shoes off.

'*And* you've got a girlfriend,' said the goth girl, smiling sweetly now. 'In fact, you didn't stop talking about her. Would you like a coffee?'

Owen shook his head. That throbbing pain again, and a sudden, violent stab of nausea. 'Um...'

Work. The word exploded in his brain like a firework, like it was lit up in neon or carved in bloody great big stone lettering. Work.

'Actually... I've probably got to make a move. I've got work.'

'Work? When?'

He looked at his watch. It was nine o'clock. And his shift started at half ten.

'An hour and a half,' he said, quietly. 'Where am I?'

The goth girl laughed. 'Cathays. I just told you.'

Owen sighed. Cathays. Just outside the city centre. It could have been worse. It could have been Swansea. He was still struggling to piece together the last few hours of the night. There had been the Cross Inn and, at some point after two or three pints, the urge to grab a takeaway and a video had left him, and they were in a taxi and heading into town. That was when it started to get just a little hazy.

But Cathays wasn't too far. It was further away from the hospital than his flat and, thinking about it logically, going home first was no longer an option, which meant he'd have to go in wearing the same clothes he'd worn the day before, but that wasn't the end of the world.

'Can I use your shower?' he asked.

The goth girl nodded. 'Top of the stairs, first on the right. There's towels in the airing cupboard.'

Owen lifted himself up from the sofa with a nauseous groan and tiptoed out of the living room, nodding a wordless 'thank you' to the goth girl before climbing the stairs.

It was while he stood under the hot spray of the shower that further fragments of information came back to him. The trawl around Cardiff's coolest bars and a few that weren't so cool before they wound up in Metros nightclub. They'd looked a bit out of place, Owen and his fellow doctors, all of them in their Ben Sherman shirts and shoes, while around them kids with spiky multicoloured hair and piercings, most of them dressed from head to toe in black, bounced around to System Of A Down and Green Day.

Lloyd had started talking to another goth girl, the girl he assumed was Kirsty, and then introduced him to Kirsty's friend, the girl who was now downstairs in Hello Kitty pyjamas. Quite what Lloyd was playing at he wasn't sure; perhaps angling for some kind of orgy; Owen could never tell with Lloyd.

Whatever his game was, Lloyd had persuaded Owen to join them in the taxi back to Cathays, stopping at a kebab shop en route. He'd tried eating the kebab in the back of the cab, and the driver had shouted something at him about no food and drink in the car. That was when Owen had dripped chilli sauce down his front. It was a little sketchy after that – a drunken conversation on the sofa; the goth girls rolling spliffs, and then nothing. He'd blacked out pretty quickly.

As Owen left the bathroom, he knocked on the door that was signposted 'KIRSTY'S ROOM' by a brightly coloured wooden plaque, and said, 'Lloyd… It's Owen. Come on, mate. We've got to go to work.'

He heard a groan and a giggle from inside the room; the groan Lloyd's, the giggle Kirsty's.

'Not me, mate,' said Lloyd. 'I've got the day off.'

'Bloody typical,' thought Owen. 'He drags me into town, gets me pissed, and then he's got the day off. Bloody typical.'

'Do you *really* have to go to work?' the goth girl in pyjamas asked as he returned to the living room to put on his shoes.

'Yeah, kind of,' said Owen. 'I'm a doctor.'

Minutes later, he stepped out into the very bright and very cold light of day. He needed food, but there wasn't time to buy any. He also needed to find his bearings. He hadn't lived in Cardiff all that long, and much of the city was still new to him.

Added to his geographical disorientation was the feeling of shame, as he made his way past pensioners pushing trolleys and commuters on their way to work. It was as if they all knew *exactly* what he'd done the night before, as if they could see right through him. Or maybe they could just smell the booze as he walked past. Either way, it wasn't a good place to be.

The bus journey was marred by screaming toddlers, which he really didn't need as that headache began to kick back in. He could have phoned in sick, of course, but that wasn't really an option. Doctors don't 'do' sick days. Doctors, according to unwritten law, have immune systems that can defeat any virus, and they most definitely do not have hangovers.

He got to A&E at the hospital almost an hour after he had left the goth girl's house. His colleagues and so-called friends were waiting for him, all with grinning faces or pursed lips.

'Tut, tut, tut… Where did you get to last night, you dirty stop-out?'

'Feeling a bit worse for wear?'

'Is that kebab sauce you've got down the front of you?'

'I think Dr Harper's going to need a lie down. Shame we need him over on 5. Grab a coffee, and put on a jacket. Can't have you walking around looking like a bloody tramp. You're coming with me.'

The first patient he had to see was a young boy who had been hit by a car on his way to school. When his superior, Dr Balasubramanian (Dr Bala, for short), pulled the curtain aside, Owen felt his heart sink. He could deal with all aspects of the job; the blood, the injuries, the bodily fluids; but it was always hard when it was a child. Luckily he'd not had to deal with too many of them, and all the kids he'd dealt with had left the hospital breathing.

'Dr Harper, this is Darren. Darren, this is Dr Harper. He's just going to take a look at you, to find out what we need to do to make you better.'

Darren Lucas was nine years old and somebody's blue-eyed boy, but now he was lying in a hospital bed, crying every time he moved. Just looking at him, Owen could tell he had a broken arm, perhaps a broken collar bone. They'd need to run him through a CT scan and a chest X-ray. He talked in hushed tones with Dr Bala, running through procedure, and Dr Bala nodded, and added a few suggestions, as he always did. When he'd finished the consultation, Owen turned to Darren.

'You're gonna be OK, Darren,' he said, smiling softly. 'We'll have you playing football in no time.'

'I hate football,' said Darren, between sobs.

'OK,' said Owen, 'well, whatever it is you like playing.'

He leaned a little closer to the boy.

'Listen, mate. I know it's scary and I know it hurts, but you're gonna be fine. OK? D'you trust me?'

Darren Lucas nodded.

'You're being very brave, Darren. You carry on like this and we might have to give you a medal.'

Darren smiled, before another jolt of pain caused him to wince.

'You know, we have nurses for that,' said Dr Bala, as they walked away from Darren's cubicle.

'What do you mean?' asked Owen.

'Friendly patter. We reassure, but you don't have to go overboard on the nice-doctor act.'

'It's not an act. I just think how would I feel if I was in their shoes. It must be pretty bloody scary. Big hospital. Lots of doctors talking incomprehensible gibberish.'

'Yes, I know that, and don't think I'm indifferent to it, but you do have to maintain just a little bit of distance sometimes. It's a lot of hard work, you know.' Dr Bala laughed and gave Owen a hefty pat on the shoulder, another of his trademark gestures. 'Now the other patient I'd like you to take a look at is the gentleman in 7. Very strange, this one. Came in fifteen minutes ago. One of the ambulance drivers found him outside the main doors.'

They approached the bed of the next patient, a young man no older than twenty-five. He was covered in soot and black ash, but not burned in any way. He was shirtless, and a dressing had been applied to a wound on his chest.

'Who are you?' the young man asked.

'This is Dr Harper,' said Dr Bala. 'Dr Harper, this is Michael. Michael, would you care to tell Dr Harper what you just told me, about your accident?'

'It wasn't an accident,' said Michael, solemnly. 'It *wasn't* an accident. They were bombing us. They were bombing the city. I couldn't stop it. The bombs just kept falling.'

'And when was this, Michael?'

Michael said simply: '1941.'

Dr Bala turned to Owen and surreptitiously raised one eyebrow.

'Michael was on Neville Street, in Riverside, during the Blitz.'

'Where am I now?' Michael asked. 'I was dreaming, wasn't I? It was a dream?'

'That may well be the case,' said Dr Bala. 'That may very well be the case. Could you tell Dr Harper your date of birth?'

'Yes. First of April, 1929.'

Dr Bala turned to Owen again. '1929,' he said. 'Michael tells me there was some sort of accident, in 1953, and that he then found himself in 1941 during the Blitz.'

'Stop talking like that,' said Michael. 'Like I'm… like I'm gone in the head.'

His voice shook and his eyes filled with tears.

'I just want to wake up,' he said. 'I just want to wake up again, back home. I just want this to stop.'

'OK, Michael. I'll send one of the nurses in shortly. We'll help you,' said Dr Bala, before putting one hand on Owen's shoulder and steering him away from the cubicle.

'Well?' he said.

'Schizophrenia?' said Owen. 'I mean… Paranoid delusions, displacement… That's probably schizophrenia, isn't it?'

'Not our problem to diagnose, but I reckon it's a good guess. What would you do?'

'What do you mean?'

'Well, what would be your next course of action? His injuries were very slight. The wound on his chest… a splinter of wood… was superficial and has been treated.'

'Check for concussion?'

'Yes. Already done. What next?'

'Call in psych.'

'Good. And…?'

'You want the honest answer?'

'Of course.'

'I'd send him to St Helen's Psychiatric. No reason to keep him in here if he's been treated, and he's as mad as a bucket of frogs.'

'Quite. Though I'm not sure I would have used your vernacular.'

Owen paused. What had happened to that empathy they were just talking about? Now here he was half-joking about somebody's madness, when it was clear the guy was scared out of his mind. What he was saying might not be true, but it was clearly true to him.

'Do you reckon he'll be OK?' asked Owen.

'What do you mean?'

'Well, at St Helen's. I mean, what happens to him next?'

'Chances are he was already being cared for in some capacity, or he has family who are worried sick about him. It's unlikely he'll have to remain there in the long term. The important thing, Owen, is that the moment he walks out of that door you forget all about him. It's not easy, I know it's not, but it's important. If you're a doctor for any length of time you'll get to see hundreds of patients like him, equally out of their minds, equally distraught. You can't go worrying about all of them.'

'You met him?' asked Toshiko.

Owen nodded.

They were in the Autopsy Room, Owen leaning back against the far wall.

'I couldn't say anything. I… I didn't know what to say. What if *I'm* the reason he's here? And it wasn't just that, it was something else…'

'What?'

Owen took in a deep breath, sighed, and shook his head.

'It's stupid, really. I mean really, really stupid. I was a doctor for how long? Saw everything on the wards. You name it, I saw it. People coming in who you'd barely recognise as human, let alone alive. Burns, car crashes, stabbings, shootings. We had it all.'

'What are you talking about?'

'It was that day,' said Owen. 'It was the same day. One minute I'm talking to Darren Lucas, this kid who's been run over, then I'm talking to Michael, the crazy guy who's been to 1941. I was talking about Michael all afternoon, to the other doctors, and the nurses. I'd almost forgotten about Darren.' He paused. 'He was only nine.'

Owen rubbed his eyes with his forefinger and thumb and walked away from his desk.

'I worked a twelve-hour shift that day,' he said. 'The boy… Darren… he had to wait God knows how long for one of his scans, but I popped in to see him a couple of times, and he seemed OK. His parents were worried sick, but I told them everything was going to be fine. And then, just before they were going to take him up for the scan, he died. Just like that.'

Owen closed his eyes and shook his head.

'It was a blood clot. Something we hadn't picked up; *couldn't* have picked up. I had to go and tell his parents. I'll never forget the look in their eyes…'

He paused again, rubbing both eyes with the palm of his hand.

'Darren Lucas. The funny thing is, you get so many patients, and you forget their names eventually, but I never forgot Darren's. I forgot all about Michael. There were dozens more nutters over the years; you can't remember all of them. But now he's back. It must be my fault. It must be something I've done, something I've screwed up. He comes to me all those years ago and now he's back, here, now.'

Toshiko went to him immediately, putting her arms around him. There was a moment, just a moment, when they looked into each other's eyes and neither of them was entirely sure what the embrace meant.

Toshiko broke away suddenly.

'I'm sorry,' she said. 'But trust me, Owen. It's not just you.'

FIVE

The fireworks exploding over the River Dojima reminded her of flowers. Like great big burning flowers of pink, and blue, and green. Toshiko Sato's father held her in his arms while behind them, on the river itself, the boats made their way out towards the point where the Dojima meets the Okawa, each one carrying dozens of people, all of them dressed in brightly coloured costumes.

'Smile!' said her mother, and Toshiko and her father beamed for the lens in the seconds before they were both near-blinded by the flash.

The Tenjin Festival was Toshiko's favourite time of year, better than the Cherry Blossom Festival, or the Aizen Festival. Better, even, than the Midosuji Parade, and she *loved* the Midosuji Parade.

It was only during the festivals that her father ever seemed to have time for them. It wasn't his fault, as her mother often reminded her. Her father was a very busy man with a very important job, and he often had to travel far away, but he never missed the Tenjin Festival.

When the procession of the boats was over, Toshiko's parents walked her back through the city streets, each holding her hand. They stopped at a stall where her father bought her a bag of wagashi sweets, and then they walked down to the nearest subway.

The train was busy, thanks to the festival, and Toshiko spent all of her journey on the Yotsubashi Line surrounded by a forest of people's legs. She held on tightly to a nearby bar and tried not to stumble when the train stopped suddenly in each station. It was a little quieter on the Midosuji Line, but even so she still had to sit on her mother's lap.

By the time they got to their stop, Toshiko was asleep and had to be carried up the steps to their apartment, which overlooked Minami, in the south of the city. On clear days, which didn't come very often, you could see out past the city to the bay of Osaka, and her father had told her that on some days you could even see Kobe, though she didn't believe him.

She woke as her father opened the door and they stepped into the apartment, her mother and father kicking off their shoes. As her mother carried her through to her room, they passed the door to her grandmother's bedroom, and she could hear her grandmother snoring, as she did almost every night. In the mornings, of course, when her mother or father would say something about the snoring, Grandma would deny it, saying they must have been imagining it, which was a source of endless amusement for Toshiko and her parents.

Her mother tried to put her to bed and turn out the light but, having slept for much of the subway journey, Toshiko was restless and wanted a bedtime story.

'All right,' said Toshiko's mother, eyeing her suspiciously. 'You can have a story, but just the one. It's way past your bedtime. Which story would you like? Tin-Tin? The fairy tales?'

'Fairy tales!' said Toshiko, suddenly very much awake, clapping her hands together and bouncing up and down on her bed.

'OK… Fairy tales it is,' said her mother, picking the book from Toshiko's shelf and sitting on the edge of the bed. She opened the book, and began to read.

'This story is called "The Land Of Perpetual Life". Many, many years ago, there lived a rich man called Sentaro. His father had been a powerful and wealthy man, and Sentaro inherited his fortunes from him, but he was not hardworking like his father, and spent his time being idle and lazy.

'One day, when Sentaro was thirty-three years old, he thought of death and sickness, and the thoughts made him very sad.

'"I would like to live until I am six hundred years old, at least," said Sentaro, "so that I am never sick and I am never old. The span of a man's life is far too short."

'Sentaro had heard stories of people who lived much longer than normal men, and indeed women, such as the Princess of Yamato who, so he'd been told, lived to the ripe old age of five hundred. He had heard stories, too, of a mighty Chinese emperor called Shin-no-Shiko, who had built the Great Wall of China. Despite his riches, his palaces, and his precious stones, Shin-no-Shiko was unhappy because he knew that one day he would die.

'Every day when he woke up, and every night when he went to sleep, Shin-no-Shiko would pray that somebody might give him the famous Elixir of Life—'

'What's an elixir?' asked Toshiko.

'It's like a drink,' said her Mum. 'A drink that makes you live for ever.'

'OK.'

'So… Where was I? Oh yes. He prayed that somebody might give him the famous Elixir of Life.

'Then one day a courtier, whose name was Jofuku, told him that far, far away across the sea, on Mount Fuji, there lived hermits who possessed the Elixir of Life, and that whoever drank it would live for ever.

'Shin-no-Shiko told Jofuku to travel to Mount Fuji, find the hermits, and bring back with him a bottle of the magical elixir. He gave Jofuku his best boat, and a chest filled with his finest jewels and bags full of gold, for him to give as gifts to the hermits.

'Jofuku sailed away across the sea, but he never returned. It was said, however, that the hermits on Mount Fuji now worshipped Jofuku as their patron god.

'Hearing of this story, Sentaro was determined that he would find the hermits and, if he could, join them, so that he might have the water of perpetual life.

'He travelled for many days and many nights, until

he reached Mount Fuji, but there were no hermits to be found. All that remained on the mountain was the shrine of Jofuku. As he had travelled for so long, Sentaro prayed for seven more days, pleading for Jofuku to show him the way to the hermits and their elixir.

'On the night of the seventh day, as Sentaro knelt inside the temple, a door opened with a great big BANG!'

Her mother yelled the word, and Toshiko jumped and then giggled.

'And from out of the door came the spirit of Jofuku, like a glowing puff of smoke.

'"Sentaro!" said Jofuku. "You are a selfish man and your wish cannot easily be granted. Do you really think that you would like to live as a hermit? Hermits can only eat fruit and berries and the bark of pine trees; a hermit cannot live amongst others, amongst family or friends, and must live by many rules. The hermit does not feel hunger, or pain. You, Sentaro, live well. You eat fine foods, and drink much sake. You are not like other men, for you are lazy, and when it is cold you complain that it is too cold, and when it is hot you complain that it is too hot. A hermit does not do these things. Do you think that you could *really* live as a hermit?

'"However, as you have prayed now for seven days and seven nights, I will help you in another way. I will send you from Mount Fuji to the Land of Perpetual Life, where nobody dies, and where everyone lives for ever!"

'And with that, Jofuku placed in Sentaro's hand an origami crane, and he told him to sit on the back of the crane, so that it could carry him to this faraway land.

'Sure enough, when Sentaro sat on the crane it grew and grew and grew until it was bigger than any normal crane, and then it carried him away, over the top of Mount Fuji, and out over the big blue sea.

'They flew across the ocean for many thousands of miles, Sentaro and the paper bird, until they reached a faraway island. When they landed on this island the origami crane folded itself up and flew straight into Sentaro's pocket.

'Sentaro walked around the island, and saw that the people there were prosperous and wealthy, and so he settled at a hotel in one of the villages. The owner of the hotel, a kindly man, spoke with the governor of the island and arranged for Sentaro to be given a house of his own, so that he could live for ever in the Land of Perpetual Life.

'And it was true what Jofuku had said, for in the Land of Perpetual Life nobody ever died or got sick. People came to the island from all around, from China and India and even faraway Africa, and told the people on the island about a land called Horaizan, where everybody was eternally happy, but the only way to reach this land was by travelling through the gates of death.

'Unlike Sentaro, the people of the island were not afraid of dying. In fact they longed for it, so desperately did they want to experience paradise. They were tired of their long, long lives, and wished to live in Horaizan instead.

'But nothing could help them. When they drank poisons, unlike you or me, the people in the Land of Perpetual Life did not get sick or die, but carried on living, even healthier than before. The people there would eat the poisonous globe fish in their restaurants, and even sauces made from Spanish flies…'

'Ewww…' said Toshiko. 'Flies? That's horrible!'

'That's right. Spanish *flies*. But they were never sick and they never died. Sentaro could not understand it. He thought that he would enjoy living for ever, and so he was the only happy man on the island.

'After many years, however, Sentaro realised that living for ever was not as enjoyable as he had thought it would be. He wasn't always happy, and things did not always go to plan. Sometimes, in fact, life was very hard and not much fun at all, and nothing ever seemed to change.

'Sentaro prayed to Jofuku once more, to take him away from this terrible place and, all at once, the origami crane leapt from his pocket, spread its wings and flew him swiftly away from the island and across the sea to Japan.

'They were halfway across the sea when they flew into a storm. The magical paper crane was soaked through, and its paper began to crumple. Soon enough it could no longer fly, and it fell into the sea with a SPLASH! and took Sentaro with it.

'Terrified that he might drown, Sentaro cried out for Jofuku to save him, but no rescue came. As he struggled to stop himself from sinking, he saw a terrific SHARK! swimming in the waters nearby. It drew nearer, and nearer, and NEARER!

'"Help me, Jofuku! Help me!" cried Sentaro as the shark opened it's great big jaws wider and WIDER!'

Toshiko now hid her face behind her mother's arm,

so that she couldn't even see the illustration of the shark inside the book.

'Suddenly Sentaro awoke and found himself lying on the floor of Jofuku's shrine on Mount Fuji. He realised that all of his adventures in the Land of Perpetual Life had been nothing but a dream.

'As he thanked the stars and all the gods for his good fortune, a bright light came towards him, and in the light there stood a messenger. The messenger held Sentaro's hand and said, "I am sent by Jofuku who, in answer to your prayer, has given you this dream so that you could see for yourself how it would be to live in the Land of Perpetual Life, and to see how you begged to return to Japan so that you could live a natural life and then pass through the gates of death to the Land of Horaizan. You also saw, when threatened by the shark, that you were scared of death. You now fear both eternal life and death, and this is as a normal man lives. Now return to your home, Sentaro, and live a good and industrious life. Remember your ancestors, and provide for your children. Thus you will live to an old age and be happy, for when selfish desires are granted they do not bring happiness."

'And so Sentaro returned to his home, and he did as the angel had told him, and he lived a long and happy life, where he remembered his ancestors and gave to his children. Sentaro died a very old man, but he is now in the Land of Horaizan, where he lives happily ever after. The End.'

'Another one, another one,' said Toshiko, and her mother laughed.

'No, Toshiko. Not tonight. You're very tired. All those fireworks and the boats… It's been a very long day.'

Toshiko moaned and sulked, though she knew there wouldn't be another story that night. As her mother placed the book on the shelf and went to turn off the light, Toshiko's father appeared in the door.

'Have you eaten all the edamame?' he asked.

'No,' replied Toshiko's mother.

'There's none in the refrigerator. I was feeling a little hungry. Maybe your mother?'

'She doesn't like edamame.'

'Mmm.'

Toshiko's mother turned to her.

'Goodnight, Toshiko,' she said, beaming.

'Goodnight, Mum. Goodnight, Dad.'

The light went off, and the door was quietly closed, plunging the room into darkness.

As Toshiko drifted off to sleep, she thought of faraway places, like the Land of Horaizan. She liked the stories her mother told her. It felt, sometimes, as if the characters were her friends.

Osaka was such a big and noisy city and had so many people, but none of the people were like the ones in the stories her mother read. There was no magic in Osaka; only buildings, and flashing signs and subway trains. No magic, that is, until that night.

When Toshiko awoke early the next morning, there was a man in her room. Had she been any older than five, this might have filled her with terror, or perhaps a greater and deeper sense of threat, but instead the strange appearance of the man simply confused her.

'Who are you?' she asked.

The man looked scared, as if he'd seen a ghost, or perhaps the shark out of the fairy tale.

'What did you say?' he asked, in English. Toshiko could speak English. Her parents had taught her when she was little and they had lived on the other side of the world, and so she understood him.

'Who are you?' Toshiko asked, now speaking in English.

'My name's Michael,' whispered the man. 'Where am I?'

'This is Osaka,' said Toshiko, rubbing the sleep from her eyes and yawning.

'Where's Osaka?' asked Michael.

'In Japan,' said Toshiko.

Michael laughed, and put his hand over his mouth to silence himself. He started shaking his head and padding quietly from one side of the room to the other.

'Japan…' he whispered. 'I'm in Japan.'

He walked over to her window, and opened the blinds just enough so that he could see outside.

'Oh my God,' he said.

'What is it? What's the matter?' asked Toshiko.

'This… this city… It's… *huge*. It's like something out of a film. And the cars… Look how many cars there are.'

'How did you get here?'

'I don't know,' said Michael. 'I still don't know. It's like magic. But don't be scared. I'm not going to hurt you. I just need to go home.'

'Where's home?'

'It's a long, long way away.'

'Like the Land of Horaizan?'

'No. No… It's further away than that.'

Outside, in the hallway, Toshiko's parents were leaving for work. Michael looked this way and that around the bedroom, before diving inside a small, pink wardrobe and closing the doors after him. The door to Toshiko's bedroom opened, and her mother leaned into the room.

'Were you talking to yourself, Toshiko?'

'I was talking to Michael,' said Toshiko. 'He's a magic person.'

'It's those fairy tales,' said her father, standing in the hallway. 'Imaginary magic friends! Whatever next?'

'We're going to work now,' said Toshiko's mother. 'Grandma is watching television. You be a good girl and we'll see you later.'

The door closed and, as she heard her parents walk down the steps toward their cars, Toshiko said, 'It's OK, now. They've gone.'

Michael stepped out of the wardrobe. 'I need to go,' he said. 'I need to find a way out of here.'

'Why can't you use magic?'

Michael sighed. 'It doesn't work like that,' he said. 'It just happens.'

Michael's stomach made a growling noise, like the noise Toshiko's father made when he was pretending to be a lion, like in a story, and Toshiko laughed.

'Sorry,' said Michael. 'I'm hungry. I can't remember the

last time I ate properly. I took some peas in the pod from your refrigerator last night…'

Toshiko laughed. 'Those weren't peas in the pod, silly!' she said. 'They're edamame!'

'Oh,' said Michael. 'Do you have any more food I can eat? I'll eat something, and then I'll go. God knows what anyone would think if they found me here. I'd probably be strung up.'

'I have some wagashi,' said Toshiko.

'What's wagashi?'

'They're sweeties.'

Michael shrugged. Sweets would have to do when he was this hungry.

'I'll go get them,' said Toshiko. 'You stay here.'

Toshiko got out of bed, and opened her door just a little to check that the coast was clear. She could see her grandmother in the living room, sitting in her favourite armchair. She was already sleeping. Her grandmother seemed to sleep a lot, but then she was usually awake very early, pottering about on the roof garden, watering the plants and feeding the grosbeaks and doves.

Toshiko tiptoed out of her bedroom and made her way through the living room toward the kitchen. Her grandmother was snoring again and, though Toshiko wanted to laugh, she decided not to, as it might wake the old woman up. On the television was Toshiko's favourite programme, *Kagaku ninja tai Gatchaman*, or 'Science Ninja Team Gatchaman'. It was a cartoon about five superheroes who worked as a team to fight monsters. Toshiko wanted to be a member of Science Ninja Team Gatchaman.

As Toshiko slowly and quietly opened the door to the fridge and lifted out the bag of wagashi, a strange thing happened. The picture on the television began to blur and then fizz, as if the signal had been lost. The light inside the fridge flickered several times, and then there was an almighty noise, like the sound of somebody hitting a great big drum. Even so, her grandmother did not wake.

'Toshiko…' said a voice. It was a terrifying voice, the scariest thing she had ever heard; like the kind of voice a snake might have, or maybe even a dragon.

Though a part of her didn't want to, Toshiko turned around and saw, stood in the middle of the kitchen, a tall man in a black suit and bowler hat, holding an umbrella. His skin looked diseased, almost grey, and he was wearing little round sunglasses.

'I smell something sweet,' the pale man rasped, his lips curling up in a sneer to reveal teeth that looked like hundreds of needles.

'The Traveller…' he said. 'Where is he?'

Toshiko shook her head and hugged the bag of sweets close to her chest. Looking past the pale man at her bedroom door, she saw it open very slightly, and through the narrow gap she saw Michael.

The pale man had noticed none of this, and he crossed the kitchen in one swift move, clutching her by the throat and lifting her off the ground. The bag of sweets fell to the floor, spilling out its contents.

'Where is the Traveller?' said the pale man and, with one

hand, he lifted off the little round sunglasses, to reveal eyes as black as ink.

'I could kill you just by looking at you,' he hissed.

Toshiko heard Michael cry out: 'No!'

The pale man dropped her to the ground and, as she fell, she saw Michael running from her room, his face contorted with anger, his hands reaching out toward the pale man as if he were about to strangle him.

Then he was gone; Michael had vanished.

The pale man looked down at Toshiko.

'We shall see you again,' he said, and in the blinking of an eye, he too was gone.

In the living room, Toshiko's grandmother stirred. 'Toshiko?' she said. 'Toshiko? What is all that noise? Are you getting up to mischief?'

Her grandmother eased herself out of her armchair and walked to the kitchen. 'What are all those sweets doing all over the floor? No sweets before breakfast.'

'I'm sorry, Grandma,' said Toshiko. 'I'll put them back in the fridge.'

'So you see?' said Toshiko. 'It isn't just you. It's both of us. I just can't work out *how*. I'd forgotten... How could I forget *that*?'

Owen shrugged, and then looked at her with a moment's flicker of compassion. 'You must have been so scared,' he said. 'You must have *wanted* to forget.'

He sighed and paced back and forth with both hands linked over his head.

'Jack knows something,' he said. 'I can tell. Something about the way he reacted when Michael turned up. He definitely knows something. Since he came back... something's different about him. All these secrets...'

'Um, Tosh...'

It was Gwen, standing at the entrance to the Autopsy Room. Neither of them had heard or seen her arrive.

'Yes?' said Toshiko.

'I...' Gwen trailed off before she could continue her sentence, looking from Owen to Toshiko and back again.

'Did you...?' said Owen.

'Did I what?'

'Did you hear any of that?'

'Any of what?' asked Gwen.

'What we were just talking about?'

'You mean about you both having met Michael before tonight?'

Owen grimaced, and Toshiko looked down at her shoes as if in shame.

'Yep. That's the one,' said Owen.

'Yes. Yes, I did hear that.'

'Right...'

Gwen shifted awkwardly. 'Actually,' she said, 'I think it's possible we all have.'

'What do you mean?' asked Owen.

'Well, you've met him before. And I just heard what Tosh told you. And I think I've met him too.'

SIX

'Have we run out of Marmite?'

Great, thought Gwen Cooper. Man the hunter-gatherer, reduced to scouring around the kitchen asking his girlfriend if there's any Marmite left.

'I don't know, Rhys,' she replied, shouting down the hallway between their bedroom and the kitchen. 'Did we buy any?'

'I dunno,' said Rhys. 'I was going to get some the other day, but now I can't remember whether I did or not.'

He was standing in front of an open cupboard, wearing only his pants and a pair of slippers.

Man the hunter-gatherer, indeed.

Gwen wondered how the timeline of human development might look in illustrated form. It might start with monkeys dragging their knuckles across the floor, developing into upright cavemen brandishing clubs, and ending with an illustration of Rhys, in profile, standing in his pants and slippers and peering into a cupboard.

'Found some!' said Rhys. 'There was some behind the Oxo cubes in the cupboard.'

'How long's it been there, Rhys?' asked Gwen. 'It might have gone off.'

'Can Marmite go off?' asked Rhys.

It wasn't a question that Gwen wanted to bother herself with this morning, because this morning was her first day with a new partner. The last one had transferred to Bristol, and the one before that was now a desk sergeant. It almost felt like her first day on the job all over again.

'Rhys… What do you think?' she said, stepping into the kitchen. 'Do I look all right, or do I look a twat?'

Rhys looked at her and smiled, wiggling one eyebrow suggestively. 'Oh yes,' he said. 'Very fetching. Would you like to arrest me, officer? Why are you worried about what you look like?'

'Seriously, Rhys. Does it look all right?'

'It's your uniform, love. You wear it every day. It's not like you're going to a wedding.'

'I know, but it's just… Never mind.'

'You look lovely,' said Rhys. 'But then you always look lovely to me.'

Gwen smiled. 'Thanks, love,' she said.

Rhys smiled back and took a bite of his Marmite on toast. 'Funny this,' he said, with a mouthful of food. 'Sell-by date said fifth of March but it tastes fine. You'd never know.'

The corridors of the police station smelled of coffee first thing in the morning. Coffee and floor polish.

80

Sergeant Rowlands, an older man with more than a touch of the George Clooney about him (which had *not* gone unnoticed), walked her through the station, his long-legged strides leaving her struggling to keep up.

'You know who Andy Davidson is, don't you?' he said.

Gwen nodded.

'He's been with us for best part of a twelvemonth. Nice lad. Down to earth and all the rest of it. Don't get him onto the subject of TV or he'll talk your leg off.'

Gwen asked him where they would be going on patrol.

'Town,' said Sergeant Rowlands. 'It's half term, so it should keep you busy.'

He walked her into one of the staff rooms, where a tall PC with fair hair sat reading *The Sun*.

'Andy, this is Gwen Cooper who I was telling you about. Gwen, this is PC Davidson. No relation to Jim. Why don't you two get yourselves acquainted and then I want you out there saving the good people of Cardiff from the forces of evil by half nine. OK with you?'

Gwen smiled, perhaps a little bashfully. She had sworn on her first day at the station that she wouldn't turn into a twelve-year-old girl when Sergeant Rowlands cracked jokes, but it was occasionally difficult.

'So... you got a boyfriend?' Andy asked as they took a left on the corner of Duke Street, opposite the edge of the castle walls, and drove down through one of the busier thoroughfares, lined on one side by market stalls and on the other by indoor shopping malls.

'What? I mean yes,' said Gwen. Partners for all of twenty minutes, and was he already hitting on her? Was this about to get awkward?

'Oh,' said Andy, as if he could read her mind, 'I didn't mean it like… It was just the whole getting-to-know-you chit-chat thing. No. Oh God, no. No, I just meant, like, "Have you got a boyfriend? Do you have any pets? Going away on holiday this year?" You know, that kind of thing.'

'Ah,' said Gwen, laughing and relieved. 'Yes. I have a boyfriend. Rhys.'

'Cool,' said Andy. 'I have a girlfriend. Her name's Kelly. Actually…' He paused as he took the car down through a pedestrianised area, waiting for gangs of shoppers and loitering teenagers to realise there was a police car behind them. 'Actually, we've only been seeing each other three weeks. But she's all right, like.'

He paused again as he pulled the car up next to the entrance of the St David's Shopping Centre and a flower stall.

'Which reminds me… It's our three-week anniversary today, and nothing says "I like you a lot and I'd quite like to see you again" better than a cheap bunch of flowers. Hang on a sec.'

Andy jumped out of the car and ran over to the flower stall. Gwen watched him through the window, shifting awkwardly in the front passenger seat. Was this Andy's style? Her last partner had been infinitely less endearing; a woman with a face like an aggravated bulldog and little in the way of patience. Gwen wondered whether she had picked up some of her worst habits, especially when it came to patrol. When Andy came back to the car he put the flowers in the boot.

'Can't have them on the back seat,' he said. 'What would people think? So… What does Rhys do?'

'Rhys?' said Gwen. 'Oh, he works for Luckley's.'

'Luckley's?'

'Yeah. The printers.'

'He prints stuff?'

'No. He's in logistics.'

'Lorries, then?'

'Kind of.'

'Ah, right. Any kids?'

Gwen laughed nervously. Was Andy always this inquisitive? Or was he just nervously trying to generate conversation to prevent any awkward silences? She had a feeling it was the latter.

'No,' she said. 'God, no. We've just moved into a new flat, and with Rhys working all hours and my job… No. You?'

'No. God, no. Me with a kid? I'm hardly a responsible adult now, I mean, apart from my job and everything. I'm all right holding a baby for about five minutes, but then I get really nervous I'm gonna drop it on its head or something. I'm sorry… Did that come out a bit weird?'

Gwen laughed.

'I'm sorry,' said Andy. 'I'll shut up now.'

Luckily, before any awkward silence could develop, the radio crackled into life, and a voice from the station said, 'Lemur lemur seven eight, we've got a reported shoplifter at

It Girls in the St David's Centre. That's a reported shoplifter, female, approximately twenty years of age. Apparently causing a bit of trouble. What's your location? Copy?'

'This is lemur lemur seven eight,' said Andy. 'Copy that. We're there now, so we'll go check it out. Over.'

Within seconds, Gwen and Andy were making their way through the shopping centre and, as was often the case, Gwen felt acutely aware of the attention their uniforms drew. Nobody stared exactly, but everyone *looked*. Everyone adopted a slightly cagey air about themselves, as if trying to hide things, although she'd guess that most of them had nothing to hide. It was the uniform. The Kevlar jacket, telescopic truncheon and PAVA spray didn't make them any more endearing to the general public.

They could hear the disturbance outside It Girls before they reached the shop; there was a loud and almost incessant yelling, strewn with four-letter words beginning, invariably, with F and C, that had the other shoppers rubbernecking and stopping in their tracks.

Outside the entrance to the clothes shop, a girl with a pram was being restrained by a security guard while another guard, a woman, lifted items of clothing, complete with the labels, tags, and even the clothes hangers, from a bag beneath the pram.

'Can we help?' said Andy.

'Yes,' said the female guard. 'The alarms went off as this young lady was leaving the shop. When I asked if I could search her bag, she became abusive. When Rory asked her if we could search the bag, she threatened both of us.'

'I never stole nothing!' shouted the girl. 'You're lying! You're lying! You're a lying bitch!'

'Listen, calm down,' said Andy. 'Did you take anything from the shop?'

'I never stole nothing!' said the girl once again.

'There are four T-shirts, a skirt and a belt under here,' said the female guard. 'With the tags still on. And no receipt.'

'Is there anyone else with her?' asked Andy. 'Any friends or family?'

The female guard shook her head. Andy sighed.

'So that's it?' asked Gwen. 'She just has to turn up at the station? We don't arrest her?'

'You don't think I did the right thing?' said Andy, looking vaguely insulted. 'We've got her name from the ID she had in her purse, and we checked that she gave us the right address. What else could we do? There isn't a baby seat in the back of this thing, and we most certainly do not have a crèche back at the ranch. If we'd taken her down to the station we'd have had to call social services, and believe you me that can get messy. No. She comes in to the station, and if she doesn't we can go out and arrest her. She'll probably get off with a warning, anyway. Unless she's some kind of master criminal wanted by Interpol. Like Carlos the Jackal or something. Which is a bit unlikely, in all fairness.'

Gwen stared down at the dashboard pensively. She'd said nothing during the whole incident; nothing to calm the girl down, nothing to the security guards, nothing to the shop manager. She'd stood by Andy's side like a pet dog, following him around the place, taking mental notes of everything she saw and heard, terrified that if she opened her mouth she'd say something stupid.

Something felt wrong; almost like a headache; a nagging sensation she couldn't shake.

They were now driving slowly along St Mary Street, the four lanes of which cut straight through the middle of the city, linking the civic centre and the northern edges of what was once Butetown.

Whether it was the sun in their faces, or her thoughts, or their conversation, Gwen wasn't sure, but neither of them saw the man before the car hit him, or rather he hit the car, slamming into the front left wing, his arms outstretched, screaming.

He was only a young man, dressed in strangely tatty clothes; homeless perhaps; but he looked out of his mind. Andy stopped the car abruptly, and they both stepped out into the street.

'Oi, mate…' said Andy. 'Where's the fire? You OK?'

'I'll kill him,' said the young man. 'I swear, I'll kill him. The girl, the Japanese girl, he was going to… Oh my God, I've got to go back there. Where am I?'

'Whoa, whoa, whoa,' said Andy. 'Slow down a minute. Who's stealing your thoughts? What Japanese girl? What's the matter? Tell us your name.'

'What's my bloody name got to do with anything?' said the young man. 'It's Michael. My name's Michael. Are you… are you meant to be the *police* or something?'

Gwen looked from the police car, with the word POLICE

written both on its bonnet and along its doors, and back to Michael.

'Yes,' said Andy. 'We're the police. Now Michael, I want you to calm down and tell us what happened.'

'It was Japan,' said Michael. 'I was in Japan, and the city… Oh my God… The city…' He looked around himself, at the streams of traffic moving up and down the street, at the taxi cabs and buses steering their way around the stationary police car, and then he looked up at the buildings.

'Like this,' he said. 'It was like this. So many cars. But this… I *know* this street. Is this St Mary Street?'

Gwen nodded.

'Wait…' said the young man, looking at Gwen, 'I know you. You were in that place. Under the ground. I *know* you… No puzzle too puzzling, you said.'

Andy looked at Gwen, who shrugged and shook her head. 'So…' he said, a trace of scepticism in his voice, 'you were in Japan? When exactly was this?'

'Just now,' said Michael. 'Ten seconds ago. Just *now*. There was a man, in a bowler hat. He had… Oh, God… He had these teeth, and these eyes… And the girl…'

Keeping one hand on Michael's shoulder, Andy turned to Gwen and whispered, 'We'll need to take him in if he's in this state. Probably Care in the Community. But he's a liability out here, so if you radio back to the station and tell them we're bringing him in, they can get on the blower to a psychiatrist. Saves us faffing about back at the station.'

Gwen nodded sheepishly and dived back into the car.

There was a trick to unlocking the door to their flat, but be damned if she'd managed to work it out yet. Every day, without exception, she'd find herself getting increasingly frustrated, wiggling the key from left to right, and then up and down. Trying not to push the key all the way in. Pulling the door back towards the door frame and pushing it away. Eventually, as was usually the case, Rhys opened the door for her from inside.

'Having trouble?' he asked. 'You know, you'll be buggered if I'm ever away somewhere when you get home.'

'Ha ha, very funny,' said Gwen, sarcastically.

'So…' said Rhys, 'how was your day?'

'Don't,' said Gwen. 'I don't want to talk about it.'

Rhys followed her through to the living room, where Gwen kicked off her shoes and threw her jacket over the back of one of the chairs at the dining table.

'Why not?' he asked.

'Because it was rubbish,' said Gwen, dropping herself down onto the sofa and putting her head in her hands. '*I* was rubbish. I was just rubbish.'

'What do you mean, "rubbish"?'

'I mean I was rubbish,' said Gwen. 'I just followed Andy, my new partner Andy, I followed him around like this stupid bloody… *toddler* or something. Something was wrong. Everything that came up, I just froze. I didn't know what to do. I just *stood* there. I was useless. I was worse than useless. I was *rubbish*. I don't know what was wrong with me…'

Rhys sat down next to her and put one arm around her

shoulder. He stroked her hair and then pulled gently on her earlobe.

'You weren't rubbish,' he said. 'You *aren't* rubbish. You just had an off day.'

'Rhys, how long have I been there now? It shouldn't have been like today. It was like something was nagging at me all day. Like I had something else on my mind, but I can't work out what it was. Maybe I'm not meant to be doing this.'

Rhys looked at her, wide-eyed.

'Oi, now…' he said. 'None of that. You're good at your job. And it's what you've *always* wanted to do.'

Gwen nodded, tearfully. 'Apart from when I was six,' she said with a crumpled smile. 'When I was six I wanted to be She-Ra.'

Rhys laughed and, leaning forward, he kissed her on the cheek and then the lips. 'I believe in you,' he said, running his hand through her hair and smiling. 'You're so brave, doing what you do. I couldn't do it. I'd never pass the physical, for one thing!' He laughed. 'Did I ever tell you you're my hero?'

'Oh God,' said Gwen, pulling away from him and laughing. 'Bette Midler? Rhys… Are you trying to tell me something?'

Rhys laughed, falling back into the sofa. He looked at her again and smiled.

'I mean it,' he said. 'I'm so bloody proud of you.'

'We've all met him,' said Gwen. 'I knew I'd seen him somewhere before. You see so many faces, and you forget most of them. It wasn't until I heard what Tosh said. It suddenly made sense. We thought he was nuts…'

'So did we,' said Owen. 'Well, who wouldn't?'

'But why us?' asked Gwen. 'Why did he turn up in *our* pasts? And what about Ianto? And Jack?' She turned to Toshiko. 'The man in the bowler hat?' she said. 'It was real?'

Toshiko shrugged. 'I don't know,' she said. 'I'd forgotten everything until tonight. At first… when I saw Michael… I just thought it was, you know, déjà vu or something. Like I knew his face from somewhere, but I couldn't place it. But then… suddenly I remembered everything. All I know is that it felt real at the time, and if I think about it, I can hear that… that *thing's* voice, and I can smell its breath. It was just horrible.'

'So something's coming for him,' said Gwen. 'Michael said he'd seen a man in a bowler hat. Tosh, you've seen that too. Something's coming for him.'

'And I've got one other question,' said Owen, gravely. 'How do we even know we can trust him?'

SEVEN

Basement D-4, according to the files, had been completed in January 1942. The other storage areas had been running out of available space, and Torchwood had first looked into hiring private contractors to construct a further two large storage spaces as early as 1910.

It had been a large-scale operation, building such spaces so deep underground, and the construction firm was paid handsomely. It was 1915 when work first began on the auxiliary areas, and Torchwood had informed the firm that the entire facility was a part of Britain's war effort, and as such should not be discussed with anybody.

This was not necessarily untrue, of course. Many pieces of technology stored in Torchwood Cardiff would go on to assist, in whatever small way, Britain's role in the Great War, and there were items brought back from the battlefields of Europe which, belonging to neither the Entente nor the Central powers, were also kept there.

By the beginning of the Second World War, the two

new areas had been filled to capacity, and so a further two were constructed between 1941 and 1942 in the same part of the Hub, known then as Level D, once more under the smokescreen of serving a role in the war effort. Basement D-3 was filled with 'materials' by 1949, and so D-4 came into use.

'Well, this is all very fascinating,' said Owen, sitting back in his seat and giving an exaggerated yawn. 'Although I'm sure a potted history of Torchwood could have been included in my training, and saved me the bother of doing this n—'

'Wait… I've got something,' said Toshiko, sitting at the neighbouring workstation, and pointing at a screen. 'Audit, March 1954. Looks like they carried out an audit of everything they had in storage. It took five of them the best part of a month. That's a lot of alien toys to count.'

'I'm not sure I'm following you.'

'Here,' said Toshiko, touching the screen. 'It's a catalogue of everything that was collected before March 1954. Michael said he was helping to unload a crate, and that the crate exploded. Don't you think it's likely that if something out of the ordinary was in that crate it would have been brought here?'

Owen glanced across at her and nodded appreciatively. 'That's some good lateral thinking there, Tosh,' he said. 'I bet you're good at crosswords.'

'Actually, I hate crosswords,' said Toshiko. 'But I'd really like to see what's in that basement.'

'Tosh?'

'Yes, Owen?'

'Do you ever feel like a character in *Scooby Doo*?'

Toshiko laughed. They were walking down the steps toward Basement D-4, or rather they were treading very carefully. The lighting in this part of the facility was poor; fluorescent tubes that hadn't been changed in many years, only some of which still worked. Most of them were grimy or encrusted in cobwebs and dead moths.

'Sometimes,' she said. 'So who would you be?'

'Oh, Fred, definitely,' said Owen.

'Really? I was thinking you remind me more of Shaggy.'

'Yeah?' said Owen. 'Well, you know what they say. Shaggy by name, shaggy by nature.'

'What about me, then?' asked Toshiko. 'And if you *dare* say Velma, I'll—'

Toshiko had modified one of her counters to specifically target the electromagnetic wave she'd traced to both Michael and the basement, and it suddenly began to crackle a little louder.

'It's weaker than the reading I'm getting off Michael,' she said. 'I've never seen anything like this. As far as I can make out, it's like a kind of radiation which is harmless to humans...'

They were now standing before the entrance of Basement D-4. Toshiko punched the code into the security panel, and the door opened for the second time that night.

'Ladies first,' said Owen, peering cautiously into the gloom.

'Oh,' said Toshiko, 'you really are a gentleman.'

She walked into the storage area, and Owen followed.

'November 1953,' said Toshiko. 'There was only one acquisition that month. No real description of it, except to say that it was an artefact discovered on a British polar expedition. The source was unknown. The records say it was originally meant to be kept here on a temporary basis, after being shipped in directly from the Arctic. They were supposed to keep it here for initial tests before transferring it to Torchwood in London, but that didn't happen.'

Three of the room's walls housed eighty individual doors, like the doors of a locker, and in each door there was a keyhole.

'We're looking for container two-three-seven,' said Toshiko.

They began checking the numbers on each door, until eventually Owen said, 'I've got it.'

He pointed into an upper corner, at a locker door that was eight feet off the ground.

'Great,' said Toshiko. 'Did you bring a stepladder?'

Owen raised a sardonic eyebrow.

'OK,' said Toshiko. 'You'll have to be my stepladder.'

'What?'

'I'll climb onto your back…'

'How much do you weigh?'

Toshiko scowled at him. 'What sort of a question is that?'

'Well, if you're going to climb on me…'

'I'm not *that* heavy.'

'I'll get a ladder…'

'I'm not *that* heavy, Owen. Come on, it's the only way. It's hardly going to work the other way around, is it?'

'Hey… I'm not *that* heavy.' Sighing and shaking his head, Owen stood before the wall full of containers, and braced himself ready for her to climb onto him.

Toshiko looked around the room, as if expecting somebody to be watching them, and jumped up onto his back.

'Whoa, easy,' gasped Owen. 'What do you think this is, a bloody rodeo?'

Toshiko stretched out with the key. 'I can't reach it,' she said.

'I'll go find a ladder,' said Owen, turning already, as if about to walk out with Toshiko still on his back.

'Rubbish,' said Toshiko. 'I'll get up on your shoulders.'

'What?'

'Just turn back around and I'll get up on your shoulders.'

Sighing, Owen did as she said, and with both hands pushing down on his head Toshiko climbed up onto his shoulders. He wobbled from side to side to get his balance but eventually stood firm.

Toshiko leaned forward again, and this time found that she could reach the container, sliding the key into the lock and turning it. The door opened. Toshiko felt a wave of warm air, and she could smell something, a static charge perhaps, like the aftermath of a thunderstorm.

She reached into the locker. Inside there was a wooden

box, on which the label 'ITEM 4797 24/11/53' had been stamped. She held the box with both hands and slid it back towards the open locker door, pushing out a cascading shower of dust in its wake.

'You'd better hope I don't sneeze,' said Owen.

'It's really heavy,' she said.

'How heavy?'

'Really, really heavy.'

The box rested on the edge of the locker. Just one simple lift, thought Toshiko, just like picking up a television, put the weight against your chest...

As she pulled the box free of the locker, it quickly became apparent that it was even heavier than she'd thought. The sudden addition of the extra weight sent Owen stumbling back. The box fell to the ground with a loud crash, and both Owen and Toshiko fell flat on the floor.

'Ow!' said Toshiko. 'I landed right on my coccyx.'

Owen giggled.

'You said co—'

'It's not funny,' said Toshiko. 'I'm in quite a lot of pain, actually.'

They both looked at where the box had fallen. The box itself was now smashed beyond repair, its splinters scattered around the room. The artefact lay exactly where it had fallen, on top of a floor tile that was now cracked in half.

'How *heavy* is that thing?' said Owen.

'I told you. Very.'

'Not as heavy as you, I bet...'

'Hey!'

It was a metal sphere, about the same size as a football. At first it appeared quite smooth, but as they both crawled closer towards it they saw that it was covered with finely detailed engravings. One side of the metal ball was cracked open, but neither of them could see what was inside.

'Did we just do that?' asked Owen

'No,' said Toshiko. 'Look around the edges of the crack. It's melted, like something burnt its way out from inside.'

Owen climbed the stairs into the Hub, holding the metal ball to his chest. He liked to think he had a certain youthful athleticism, but even so he was exhausted. The ball must have weighed forty kilos, at least, and it was a long walk from Basement D-4 to the Hub.

Gwen and Ianto were at their workstations, their eyes fixed upon the screens. On a third screen, between the two stations, there was a CCTV image of Michael sleeping in the Boardroom.

'What's Michael sleeping on?' Owen gasped, still struggling with the weight of the ball.

'Inflatable mattress,' said Ianto, turning in his chair. 'Left over from our camping trip. One of the few things that didn't get trashed. I couldn't find the pump, so Gwen blew it up. She's got a set of lungs on her, that girl.' He pointed at the metal ball. 'Is that a present for me?' he asked.

'Not quite, no.' Owen wheezed. He got as far as the nearest table and put the ball down. It landed on the surface with a heavy thud. 'So while I've been slogging my guts out carrying that thing up the bloody stairs, what have you two been doing?'

'Michael said there were two men,' said Gwen. 'Cromwell and Valentine. They visited him in the hospital. Asked him some weird questions. We've been trying to find out who they were.'

'Any joy?' asked Toshiko.

Gwen nodded. 'There was nothing on our database for Valentine, so I did a cross-check of all data from 1953. Much more joy.'

She span back so that she was facing the screen.

'Kenneth James Valentine. Born 1921 in Newport. Worked as a carpenter from the age of fifteen until 1941, when he joined the Royal Dragoon Guards. Was present during Operation Overlord, otherwise known as D-Day, when as part of the Twenty Seventh Armoured Brigade he took part in the landings on Sword Beach. Was injured in combat and shipped back to Britain where he spent the remainder of the Second World War convalescing. Joined the Cardiff Borough Police in 1947, and then… Well, that's it.'

'That's it?' said Owen. 'What happened? Did he die?'

Gwen shook her head. 'There's no record of him being paid by Cardiff police after 1950, but there's no death certificate. Nothing. He just vanishes.'

'And what about Cromwell?'

Gwen turned to Ianto. Ianto looked from Gwen to Toshiko and Owen. He seemed cagey.

'I kind of already knew,' he said quietly.

'What do you mean?' asked Gwen. 'What did you already know?'

Ianto pointed at his screen, and the others gathered around him. On it there was an image of a man in his mid-thirties; sharp beady eyes focused on the camera. It was a standard black and white portrait, taken in the 1950s, like a passport photograph. Next to the image there was a microfiche of his typed resume:

NAME: CHARLES ARTHUR CROMWELL
BORN: 06/03/1915
DIED: 14/02/2006
MARITAL STATUS: Divorced, no dependents
EDUCATION: Brunel Grammar School, Port Talbot,
   1926–1933
   Exeter College, Oxford 1933–1937
MILITARY etc: Royal Navy, 1938–1941, Lt Cdr
   MI6, 1941–1945
   Torchwood, 1945–1975

'Oh my God,' said Owen. 'He was one of us.'

'But what about Valentine?' asked Gwen. 'If Cromwell's file is on there, why isn't Valentine's? It's like somebody's wiped him out of existence.'

'There's one other thing,' said Ianto, turning back to his screen and pointing at the photograph of Cromwell. 'I've met this man.'

EIGHT

Looking out of the grubby windows of the DLR carriage, Ianto Jones wondered whether he would ever get to live in a swanky Docklands apartment. A place with a balcony would be nice. The kind of place where he and his friends could stand drinking fancy drinks and listening to the kind of music that people listened to when they stood on balconies and drank fancy drinks.

Maybe the new job would help. He hadn't had his first wage packet yet, but maybe a few months in this job would give him enough to get a nice apartment with an impressive view. Not yet though. For now, the elevated train would whisk him all the way from Canning Town to Canary Wharf, so that the towering apartment buildings with their balconies and their concierge service were little more than a flicker book for him to envy.

At least the job felt like something impressive. He'd wanted to work in Canary Wharf since he first moved to London and, if he was honest with himself, he'd wanted to work in a skyscraper since he was a kid. Working in a skyscraper felt like a proper job, in lieu of working in the kind of job his father would call proper, like the steelworks or fixing cars.

Canary Wharf felt like somebody had taken a little slice of New York and dropped it into the East End of London. Ianto loved the sheer verticality of this part of the city; the almost unnerving sense of vertigo he got when he craned his head back to look up at the gargantuan spires of steel and glass.

As the doors of the train opened, Ianto stepped off, buoyed by the surge of commuters, and ran down the escalators and out into Canary Wharf.

She was waiting for him near the fountains in Cabot Square.

Lisa.

'Awight, darlin'?' she said in her best 'mockney' accent. Ianto wondered whether he was blushing. He'd only known her a week, but there was something there, some kind of spark. At least he hoped there was.

'So what did you do last night?' she asked. 'Get up to much?'

'Nah,' said Ianto. 'We started a James Bondathon at my house. Just a few of the lads round.'

'A James Bondathon?'

'Yeah. We're watching our favourite James Bond films in chronological order. We're up to *Goldfinger*.'

'Sounds exciting,' said Lisa, sarcastically. 'So how's week two going so far?'

Ianto shrugged. 'OK, I guess,' he said. 'Taking a little bit of getting used to.'

Lisa laughed. 'Yeah. Tell me about it. My first month I was just freaked out most of the time. I mean, you sign all the official secrets stuff, and then... wham!'

Ianto knew what she meant. The interview had given him no clue as to what the job would actually entail. Of course, they'd told him it would be largely administrative work: filing, photocopying, answering emails, arranging meetings, that kind of thing. He'd even known that it involved classified government work, and that it was strictly hush-hush. He'd had to sign the Official Secrets Act at the interview itself, which gave him some clue as to just how secretive it might be, but the one thing nobody had cared to mention at that first interview, or indeed at any of the subsequent interviews, was aliens.

He couldn't quite describe how that piece of news had felt. He'd try and compare it to the moment when, as a child, he'd found out that Father Christmas was a myth, but he couldn't properly recall that crushing disappointment. If anything, this was like that discovery in reverse. It was as if somebody had taken him into a quiet room and told him that yes, there *was* a Father Christmas, he *did* live in Lapland, and furthermore, the company Ianto now worked for existed solely to deal with his existence.

The worst thing was knowing he'd never be able to talk about his job with his friends, but then he supposed he knew very little of what his closest friends did for a living. He knew that Gavin did something involving insurance and that Nathan worked for a travel company but, if it came down to actually describing the everyday tasks their jobs involved, he'd be stuck. Why should his job be any different?

Once they had bought a coffee and a cookie each from a Starbucks kiosk, they returned to the fountain, where they both sat on a bench. It was their morning ritual, before entering the hubbub and the organised chaos of the Torchwood Institute, or at least it had been for the last few working days.

'Oh, listen to this…' said Lisa, as if about to impart a salacious bit of gossip. 'I was talking to Tracey last night, right, and she said something weird happened while she was on the twelve-eight shift.'

Tracey was one of Lisa's colleagues on the twenty-eighth floor.

'Apparently they had a Code 200.'

'What's a Code 200?'

'It's an intruder. Somebody somehow breached all of our security, got past all the cameras, all the motion detectors, everything.'

'Really?'

'Yeah. Happened just after we left, apparently. He just turned up. Nobody knows how he got in. Tracey said they're holding him on your patch, in Information Retrieval.'

Ianto laughed. 'Yeah,' he said. 'But you know what Tracey's like. Last Wednesday she told me they'd had an actual Predator, like in the movie, down in the basement.'

'She didn't say that. She said they had pictures of

something that looked a bit like the Predator. Not an actual Predator.'

'Hang on… Should we actually be talking this loud when we're outside?'

Now Lisa was laughing. 'You're right,' she said. 'It's mental. I keep almost forgetting that nobody else knows. It's so difficult. You know, when you're on the phone to your mum and she asks you what you did in work today. I always end up saying, "Same old same old".'

'Me too,' said Ianto. 'But I always did that anyway.'

For a while they sat drinking coffee and watching the splashing waters of the fountain without saying another word. Ianto wasn't sure that he'd ever had this kind of friendship with somebody so new before, where he didn't feel the need to fill the silence, where it didn't feel like he had to keep talking. He liked it. He more than liked it.

'Come on then, Welsh Man,' said Lisa. It was the nickname she'd given him when they'd first met, during his initial training, pronouncing it in such a way that it sounded like the name of a super hero. 'Time for work. Another day, another dollar.'

'Ianto, we need to take the quarter three expenditure for Inf Ret and mark it up for the attention of Graham Evesham at UNIT. He said he needs it by eleven. Have you got that?'

The voice belonged to Ianto's line manager, Bev Stanley. It was Bev who had carried out his first interview for the job. On that occasion, she had been sweetness and light personified, but that veneer hadn't taken long to crack.

Now, just a week into his job, Ianto had come to realise that Bev only used that act in interviews. The rest of the time she was busy trying desperately to transform herself into a clone of Yvonne Hartman, the Director of Operations. She bought her clothes from the same shops, styled her hair in a rough approximation of Yvonne's, and was forever telling the others amusing or witty things that Yvonne had said to her, usually at the kind of functions she was only ever rarely invited to:

'Oh, Yvonne said the funniest thing at the Intelligence Community Awards at the Grosvenor the other night…'

'Yvonne and I were talking the other day, and she said…'

That kind of thing.

Now she was barking instructions at him, instructions that made very little sense after just six whole days of working in the department. His predecessor, a nervy guy by the name of Simon, had left under a storm cloud and had said very little to Ianto except: 'Watch Bev. She's got a mean streak a mile wide.'

He had *some* idea of what Bev was talking about. It had *something* to do with any incidents in which those who passed through Information Retrieval were also dealt with by UNIT, and the way in which the two organisations would split the costs of rendition and transferral, but other than that it was all still a mystery to him.

As he searched through the different drives on his PC for the quarter three budget, Bev stepped back out of her office.

'Oh yes, Ianto. We're expecting a visitor at some point this afternoon, from Cardiff. His name's Mr Cromwell. If he turns up any earlier, make sure you offer him tea or coffee, and if I'm away from my office call me on my mobile immediately, OK? He's to be treated like a VIP.' She paused, as if in thought. 'Actually, offer him tea or coffee *and* biscuits. And not the cheapy brand chocolate digestives, either. Give him the Hobnobs.'

Ianto suppressed a smile and nodded. When Bev's office door was closed once more, he chuckled to himself before carrying on with his work.

The staff restaurant was on the forty-eighth floor of One Canada Square, and it was possible to see the whole of the city from its windows. It was so high up, in fact, that it was possible to see *beyond* London, to the green belt that existed beyond the city limits. It made London, the sprawling metropolis, seem curiously small.

When Lisa met Ianto there, she was carrying a box of chocolates.

'Look what I've got!' she said, beaming.

'Of course,' said Ianto. 'I'd forgotten. Valentine's Day. Got an admirer, have we?'

Lisa laughed. 'No, silly. Colin gave them to me. Because I haven't had a day off sick in twelve months.'

Ianto nodded toward the box. 'So that's what we get, is it?' he said. 'For a year of good health? A box of chocolates?'

'Yeah. Well… It's better than a kick in the teeth, isn't it?'

'I suppose.'

Lisa looked down at the box. 'Authentic Belgian Chocolates,' she said, reading the packaging. 'Made in Ireland.'

They both laughed.

'So how's your morning been?' Lisa asked. 'Full of fun and laughter?'

'Yeah,' said Ianto, sarcastically. 'A laugh riot from start to finish. So are you going to open those chocolates or did you just bring them up here to show off?'

'Bit of both, really,' said Lisa. 'Hey, listen, I was talking to Tracey, and she reckons you're not the only Welsh man in Inf Ret.'

'What do you mean?'

'That man who turned up? The one who slipped past security? She said he's from Wales too.'

Ianto frowned. 'How come I work in Inf Ret and I don't know this, but Tracey works in Data Process and she does?'

'Tracey gets all the gossip.'

'So he's from Wales?'

'That's what she said.'

'Invaders From Wales?'

'Something like that. So, you want a chocolate or what?'

Ianto couldn't quite work out what the point in him signing the card was. It was a card congratulating Linda Wells on giving birth to a bouncing baby boy, Josh, 7lbs 3oz. The thing was, Linda Wells had left Torchwood over three weeks ago. He had never met her.

Even so, he felt a certain degree of pressure from the others in the office that he should sign it, especially when Martin, who sat three desks away, said, 'Simon would have signed it, but he's not here, is he?'

That then left Ianto with the quandary of what to write. He tried to think of something witty, but then realised that he didn't know Linda, and so didn't know her sense of humour. He settled on, 'Congratulations, Linda – Ianto'. No kisses. That would have been grossly inappropriate considering they'd never met.

He was handing the card back to Martin when the old man entered the office. A very old man in a long, cashmere coat and trilby hat; the kind of hat Ianto thought people had stopped wearing years ago. He walked with the assistance of a black walking stick, and it took him an age to get from the door to Ianto's desk.

'I'm here to see Bev Stanley,' said the old man. 'I'm Mr Cromwell, from Torchwood Three.'

Ianto frowned.

'Cardiff,' the old man said abruptly.

'Oh, of course,' said Ianto. 'Um… If you'd just like to take a seat… Can I get you anything? Tea? Biscuits? We've got Hobnobs.' He closed his eyes and wondered whether he was blushing. Had he *really* just asked the old man if he'd like a Hobnob?

'I'm fine, thank you,' said Cromwell. It was practically a growl.

'Oh… well… If you'd just like to take a seat… I'll call Bev now.'

He lifted his phone and called through to Bev's office, telling her that Mr Cromwell had arrived. Bev was at the door within seconds, suggesting to Ianto that, though she looked composed, she had literally dashed from her desk.

'Mr Cromwell!' she said, smiling in a way that Ianto now knew to be quite false. 'It's an honour to have you here. Really, it is. Did Ianto offer you tea or coffee?'

Cromwell nodded and made a gruff affirmative noise in the back of his throat. 'So he's here?' he asked.

'Yes,' said Bev. 'We've got him in Holding Room 4. Quite a turn up for the books. We thought at first he might be somebody else, but then he said something… We made the connection. How many years has it been?'

'Too many,' said Cromwell. 'And I'm sure I don't need to remind you of what happened last time.'

'Quite,' said Bev. 'Shall we go through and see him? I'm sure the two of you have a lot to catch up on.'

Bev walked Cromwell across the department, and through the security doors at the other end of the room. Those doors were clearance A5 and above, with A1 being the highest clearance in the organisation. Ianto was at clearance level C10.

'So what do you think that's all about?' said Martin leaning across his desk to watch them leave. 'All very mysterious. Very hush-hush.'

'It's about the intruder,' said Jason, a spotty youth who provided most of the IT back-up for Information Retrieval. 'Somebody got in here last night. S'about as much as I know.'

Ianto said nothing. He focused instead on the task of finishing a spreadsheet for the department's projected expenditure in the next quarter. It was an interminably dull job but, as he kept reminding himself, somebody had to do it and, for now at least, that somebody was him.

He had not been working for more than another fifteen minutes when the alarm rang, and a pre-recorded voice came from the overhead speakers:

'Please be aware that an emergency situation has been reported in the building. Could all staff please make their way toward the nearest exits in a calm and orderly fashion and meet at their arranged fire assembly points.'

Ianto looked at his colleagues. Each one of them had turned very pale.

'What is it?' Ianto asked. 'A fire?'

'No,' said Jason, who already had his jacket on and was walking briskly toward the doors. 'The fire alarm sounds different. This is something else.'

Ianto was the last to leave the office and, before he disappeared through the door, Martin turned to him and said, 'Come on, Ianto. We *have* to go.'

They filed out of Information Retrieval and found the concourse between the different departments on the twelfth floor already crowded with people, some of whom looked terrified, some merely bewildered.

'Has this happened before?' Ianto asked.

'Once,' said Martin, who was now sandwiched uncomfortably between two very large women. 'About two years ago. But it turned out to be nothing.'

Just as Ianto was beginning to comfort himself with the thought that once more this might be 'nothing', a terrific boom shook the building, rattling framed artworks on the walls, and causing several to stumble as they made their way toward the exits.

'Oh no…' said Martin. 'I really, really don't want to die at work. I can't think of anything worse.'

His words did little to calm the rest of the crowd, who were now in one of the stairwells. One man was trembling and pale, and Ianto noticed a woman clutching a crucifix. The pendant seemed so weirdly conspicuous in a place like Torchwood.

Ianto looked up the stairwell and saw hundreds if not thousands more staff crowding the stairs all the way up to the point where the spiralling banister reached its vanishing point. He wondered whether Lisa was anywhere in the crowd.

There was another boom, and now some of the people on the stairs began to scream.

'What about Bev?' Ianto asked. 'She was still in the holding rooms. And the old man…'

'Forget about them,' said Martin. 'They're probably safer in there than we are out here. Oh… Oh God… Don't let me die in this bloody place.'

Ianto tried to calm Martin but it was no use. He, along with many others on the stairwell, was now in a state of abject panic.

It took nearly half an hour for them to get out into Canada Square itself, and all the time the alarm was still ringing, and every few minutes what sounded like another explosion could be heard. One of the doors on a lower level had been sealed shut and had armed guards either side of it, who yelled at the staff to keep going. Ianto looked at each one briefly, and wondered whether anyone might be stuck on the other side of those doors, before he carried on walking.

Out in the square he heard someone call his name and saw, to his joy, that it was Lisa.

'Thank God you're all right,' she said. 'I was *so* worried.'

'Me too,' said Ianto. 'What's happening?'

Lisa didn't answer, as if she hadn't heard him. She simply looked at him and smiled, a smile he couldn't quite read, but which he felt the urge to mirror.

'It's a Code 200.'

Ianto looked past Lisa's shoulder and saw Tracey, smoking a cigarette and looking as if Ianto and Lisa's 'moment' was an inconvenience to her. Tracey was short and blonde, with a streak of pink in her hair and three rings in her left ear, much to the chagrin of her managers in Data Process.

'We don't know that,' said Lisa.

'Definitely a Code 200,' said Tracey. 'Apparently, if a Code 200 goes on for longer than forty-five minutes they've got the go-ahead to push the button.'

'What button?' asked Lisa, cynically.

'Self destruct,' said Tracey, evidently trying to sound matter-of-fact. 'There's a button on every floor which only A2s and above have clearance for. If a Code 200 situation can't be resolved in less than forty-five minutes, they're authorised to blow the whole building up.'

'How the bloody hell do you know all this, Tracey?' said Ianto.

'I know people,' said Tracey, tapping her nose and taking a deep drag on her cigarette. 'I am the knower of all things.'

Ianto and Lisa were about to laugh, but then they heard the sound of smashing glass and, somewhere twenty storeys up, guns being fired.

Then silence.

The alarms, the gunfire, everything fell silent, and with it too stopped the chattering of the enormous crowd that had assembled in Canada Square.

'Is that it?' said Tracey. She almost sounded disappointed.

The journey home was longer that evening, or at least it felt longer. Ianto looked out through the windows of the carriage but his thoughts didn't stray as far as envying the fancy apartment blocks or the occupants on their balconies. He thought about the day he'd had, and about the looks of anguish and panic on the faces of the people on the stairs. It had scared him. He'd never tell anyone this, of course. Who could he tell? Lisa and Tracey seemed to have taken it all in their stride.

They had been ordered to return to their offices and carry on, as if nothing had happened, but when they returned Bev was no longer there, and the door to the holding rooms was sealed off. There had been a brief period of confusion, before a man from Human Resources came down to tell them that they'd have a new manager by the end of the day. Bev Stanley's name was never mentioned again.

One or two people had taken the rest of the afternoon off, including Martin, but Ianto hadn't known what else to do apart from work.

At the flat in Canning Town, he made himself Supernoodles on toast and a cup of tea, and sat in front of the television listlessly watching the football and waiting for his flatmates to come home. They were full of stories about eccentric customers and irritating managers, and he laughed with them, but his mind was elsewhere.

At a little after seven, as was always the case on a Tuesday, his mother phoned. She asked him whether he'd eaten, and not wanting to tell her that his evening meal had consisted of Supernoodles and toast he told her he'd had sausage, beans and chips for his tea. Then she asked him how his day had been and what had happened.

'Oh you know,' he said. 'Same old same old.'

'But you didn't meet him?' Owen asked. 'Michael, I mean. You didn't actually see him?'

Ianto shook his head.

'It must have been Michael,' said Gwen. 'The visitor. The person they were talking about.'

Ianto shrugged.

'So Cromwell and Valentine were Torchwood,' said Toshiko, 'and they were tracking Michael for some time.

115

For *years*. And it all goes back to this.'

She pointed at the metal sphere that now lay on the table. The others gathered around, looking down at it.

'That's all well and good,' said Owen, 'but we don't know what *this* is. All the files say is that it was found in the Arctic. No known origin, no history, nothing. I mean, what *is* it?'

'You want to know what it is?'

They looked up from the ball and saw Jack, standing at the door of his office.

'I'll tell you what it is.'

NINE

'That,' said Jack, 'is a Vondraxian Orb.'

Owen laughed and shook his head. 'Of course it is,' he said. 'How could I forget? There's a picture of one in my Bumper Book of Orbs.' He paused. 'I'm sorry, Jack... What did you just say?'

'It's a Vondraxian Orb.'

'And what's one of those when it's at home?'

'Oh,' said Jack, crossing the Hub to the table on which the sphere lay. 'This is not at home. It's a very, very long way from home and it most certainly does not belong to us.'

Owen shrugged. 'Haven't the owners heard of finders keepers?'

'The Orb,' said Jack, 'was buried under arctic ice for almost 3,000 years before it was discovered in 1953. An expedition was launched to dig it out and return it to Britain before the Russians could get their hands on it. It was that metal ball that was inside Michael's crate. It was that metal ball which exploded the moment it was taken off the ship, killing three dockhands and leaving Michael with his, shall we say, *untimely* affliction.'

'But what *is it*?' asked Owen, losing patience.

'The Vondrax,' said Jack, 'are said to be one of the oldest sentient life forms in the universe.'

'So how come we've never heard of them?'

'Because even amongst enlightened folk such as ourselves they're like a myth, a fairy tale. The legend goes that they were born within the first few nanoseconds of the Big Bang. Tosh, you said you were picking up an electromagnetic wave, like radiation, but that it was harmless to humans?'

Toshiko nodded.

'And you said that the wave came and went, increasing in volume and then decreasing?'

'Yes, Jack.'

'That electromagnetic wave was tachyon radiation.'

'OK, Jack,' said Owen, deadpan. 'Now I know you're making this up. I did A-Level physics, and we most certainly did *not* discuss tachyon radiation.'

'You wouldn't have,' said Jack. 'Nobody here discusses tachyon radiation because nobody here knows about it. Why should you? The amount of tachyon radiation in the universe has been steadily depleting since the Big Bang. But this stuff is potent. Oh boy, is it potent…'

In the Boardroom, Michael was dreaming. He wasn't sure whether the dream was a memory or not. There were faces that he recognised, and yet he could name none of them.

Through the windows of an ambulance he saw trees. It was funny seeing them from this angle, lying flat on his back, strapped to a gurney. Only an hour ago, he would have been screaming his way through this experience, but now he was calm. He found it hard to focus, at any one moment, on any of the things that had been troubling him. He had only vague memories of the little girl in Japan and the monster that was terrorising her, or of the cities full of cars that he had seen.

He thought about the Japanese city and he could somehow recall looking out through a window in the night, and being able to see nothing but hundreds and thousands of lights. He could make little or no sense of it. What had happened to the world?

None of that mattered now, of course. In this dream, he had been given a shot at the police station, a police station that had been full of noise, bleeping sounds and people talking. There had been a group of teenagers arguing with a policeman standing behind a thick pane of glass, and they looked so strange to him; T-shirts that revealed their bellies, multiple earrings, tattoos. Was this *really* Cardiff? If he hadn't seen the Castle and the museum through the windows of the police car he would never have believed it.

But none of those things mattered to him now. Now it was as if the hard edges of the world had been sanded down and softened. The voices of those around him were barely audible, even the hum of the ambulance's engine sounded almost like a lullaby.

'Tachyon radiation,' said Jack, 'is generated when the universe is split off, when different possibilities are generated. Whenever you make a choice, that choice generates tachyon radiation. Should I have coffee? Should I have tea? Each choice generates tachyon radiation because there is now a universe in which you have coffee *and* a universe in which you have tea, but the impact those choices have on the different universes are so miniscule the amount of radiation generated is next to zilch.'

'"Zilch"? Is that a scientific term?' said Owen.

Gwen sheepishly put her hand in the air. 'Um, I know I'm kind of out of my depth here, but what has all this got to do with the Von… What were they called?'

'The Vondrax,' said Jack. 'The Vondrax, so the story goes, feed on tachyon radiation. In the first few split seconds of the universe it was in rich supply. There were so many possibilities; universes in which gravity collapses, universes in which light travels at a slower speed; and all those possibilities generated more radiation. As the universe cooled down and began to settle, those possibilities became more and more limited and localised. Tachyon radiation began to die out. The Vondrax, in their wisdom, began depositing the radiation in orbs, like this one.' Jack tapped his fingers twice on the top of the metal ball. 'They could tap into the orbs whenever they liked, *and* they could surf the tachyon radiation's electromagnetic wave to travel backwards and forwards in time. Travelling back in time meant they could alter events in the past to cause further splits, thus creating more tachyon radiation. In AD 219, the

Emperor Elagabalus entered Rome with a black sphere the Syrians worshipped as a god, the Sol Invictus. The sphere was said to have fallen from the sky. Elagabalus should never have become Emperor; he was a twisted and sadistic fourteen-year-old boy. His reign changed the course of Roman history, which generated tachyon radiation. It was all part of their plan.'

'So it's kind of like time-travel juice?' asked Gwen.

'Right,' said Jack. 'Time-travel juice, but highly concentrated time-travel juice.'

'And when it exploded…' Gwen looked at the image on a nearby monitor of Michael sleeping.

'Yes,' said Jack. 'I'm thinking maybe it was the effect the Rift had on the Orb. Rift energy and tachyon radiation are like opposing magnets; push them together and one gets forced out. That's why the Rift's been so quiet today. When the Orb exploded, Michael received a massive dose of tachyon radiation. The Vondrax can control the effects it has, but Michael… He has no say in it.'

'And these Vondrax…' said Toshiko. 'When I was a child, there was… there was this man… in a bowler hat…'

Jack nodded gravely.

He was sitting on a wooden chair, in a white room with black curtains, talking – or rather *listening* – to another doctor. To Michael, it seemed he had spent his whole life being flung from hospital to hospital, each one stranger than the last, talking to doctors.

This latest one, an Indian woman with greying hair and

a broach the shape of a lizard on the lapel of her jacket, was called Dr Hawoldar. She asked him where he lived and, when he gave her his address, one of the men from the ambulance said something about his street being demolished in the 1970s to 'make way for flats'. Michael started to laugh.

Dr Hawoldar asked him what was so funny, and Michael told her that he didn't know, that he didn't know anything any more.

'Everything is like dreaming,' he said.

'But why is he being dragged into our pasts?' asked Ianto. 'Why us?'

'We've been working in the same building as this thing for how long now?' Jack asked, tapping the ball again. 'It's broken, and most of its radiation got soaked up by Michael in the explosion, but there was still some residual radiation left in it. Close proximity to the ball, not to mention Michael, has left us all dosed with tachyon radiation. Once you've been dosed, you're always dosed – not just in the future, but in your past.'

Toshiko was on her feet now, and walking toward the table and the Orb. 'This just doesn't make any sense to me,' she said, looking down at the engraved surface of the Orb and the gaping, molten rupture in its side. 'This *thing*, can do all that? With a kind of radiation I've never heard of…'

'It's Clark's Third Law,' said Jack, raising one eyebrow and grinning.

'OK,' said Gwen, 'so assuming that this is what you say it

is, and Michael really is bouncing around in time, what can we do? For Michael, I mean.'

Jack sat on the edge of the table and shook his head. 'Nothing,' he said pensively. 'There's nothing we can do.'

'You don't know that,' said Gwen.

'No, Gwen,' said Jack, walking towards the Boardroom. 'I do.'

From the white room, he was taken to a ward in the hospital where there were many beds, and in each bed a patient. Each man's face was a mask of bewilderment or suffering, as if they were a Greek chorus of agony. Some of them were moaning, or laughing to themselves. One man was screaming. One man was singing.

The orderlies lifted Michael out of the wheelchair and lowered him onto the hard mattress of a narrow bed. He lay there for what seemed an age before Dr Hawoldar came back to him.

'Great news, Michael,' she said. 'We've just received a call from your doctor at the Torchwood Institute.'

He knew the name, but where did he know it from? *Torchwood*. He saw it as the image of a word stencilled on a wooden panel.

'Torchwood?' Michael asked. He could hear himself slurring.

'That's right,' said Dr Hawoldar. 'They said they've been very worried about you. You won't be staying here too long. One of your doctors will be here shortly.'

'When?' Michael asked.

'Soon,' said Dr Hawoldar. 'You should be back at Torchwood by three. That'll be better, won't it? Back at Torchwood with all your friends?'

Dr Hawoldar left him alone on the ward again, alone that is apart from his fellow patients, and Michael began to panic. His breathing grew heavier, and he felt his pulse begin to quicken. Torchwood. He knew the name Torchwood. He heard the growl of the car's engine as it chased him along West Bute Street; he saw an underground room filled with what looked like televisions, and the chrome base of an enormous water tower. He saw a great glass tower, like an obelisk, and a shattered mirror.

Around him, the other patients were laughing, all of them pointing at him and laughing, as if they all understood something that he didn't. Then they stopped, quite abruptly, and, as if choreographed in some way, they turned to face the far end of the ward. There, in the aisle between the hospital beds, stood three identical men, each wearing sunglasses, bowler hats and black suits and carrying umbrellas. The three men looked at Michael and smiled, each revealing teeth like hundreds of needles.

'The Traveller…' they said in unison.

That was when Michael woke up.

'It's OK,' said Jack. 'It's OK. You were having a nightmare.'

They were alone in the Boardroom.

'You,' said Michael. 'You were in that room. When I came here. You knew my name. Who are you?'

'I'm Jack Harkness,' Jack said, looking away into the far

corner of the room.

'It wasn't a nightmare,' said Michael. 'It was something else. I saw things… It was like I was seeing things that haven't happened yet.'

'It's OK,' said Jack again. 'You're here now. You're safe.'

Michael looked down and realised that Jack was holding his hand. He quickly pulled away, and looked Jack in the eye.

'I'm sorry,' said Jack. 'I didn't mean to…'

'Why do you look at me like that?' said Michael.

'Like what?'

'Like you know me. Like…' Michael trailed off and looked away from Jack, as if embarrassed. 'Like you've always known me.'

Jack stood and walked over to the far corner of the Boardroom. He could hardly bear to look at him any more. How much time did they have left? How much longer before Michael would be taken away?

'I'm sorry,' said Jack, 'I didn't mean to… I mean…'

'No, it's OK,' said Michael. 'I *feel* like I know you, but I don't. I remember things that haven't happened yet, and I'm forgetting the things that have. I don't know what's real any more.'

Jack returned to him, and held Michael's hand once more. This time Michael didn't pull away.

'This is real,' said Jack, squeezing his hand and smiling. 'Here, now. And while you're here, you're safe, with me.'

'What happens to me, Jack?' asked Michael, his eyes filling with tears. 'What happens?'

TEN

The drugs were still coursing through his veins when he came to his senses in the centre of a large loading bay, surrounded by crates and metal containers. Those senses were dulled, but he was still able to get to his feet. The feeling of disorientation passed, and slowly he began to reassemble everything that had just happened to him. There had been Japan, and the monster in the bowler hat, and then the Cardiff he didn't recognise, and the two police officers, and then the injection, and the hospital, and that name…

Torchwood.

The Indian doctor had left him alone, and then… and then… What?

Michael looked around at the crates and the containers, and at the yellow and black striped markings on the floors. The loading bay was empty.

The Indian doctor had said the name Torchwood, and then he had seen them, the men in bowler hats. They were coming for him, he knew that much and, as they walked towards him, hissing and snarling, he had been sent reeling by a violent spasm of pain, and then everything had stopped, and he had felt himself surrounded by light, before waking here.

He thought of it as waking, but how could it be waking when he hadn't slept? And yet every time it had happened that's exactly how it felt, as if everything that had gone before, from his childhood to the arrival of the crate in Tiger Bay, had been a dream.

Michael had taken no more than four steps across the loading bay when the alarm sounded, and a voice said: 'Code 200, Loading Bay 5.'

The fluorescent strip lights in the loading bay powered down, leaving just flickering orange beacon lights to illuminate the vast space like a dozen fiery strobes. The voice spoke again: 'Code 200, Loading Bay 5.'

At either end of the loading bay, roll doors suddenly flew open, spilling white light in across the darkness, and soldiers in arctic camouflage and black berets swept in, brandishing sub-machine guns.

'Don't move!' a voice yelled angrily. 'Keep your hands above your head, and do not move!'

They were getting closer now, the men with their guns, and Michael followed their orders, putting his hands in the air like he'd seen so many thieves and gangsters do in black and white films.

The red spots of laser sights bunched together like angry suns on Michael's face and chest, and he was blinded by the lights before somebody, one of the soldiers, struck him across the back of the head with the butt of their rifle.

When he came to, everything was dark. There was cloth over his face, a hood perhaps, and he was sitting, strapped into a chair. He tried to free himself but couldn't. The only sound he could hear was his own breathing.

The hood was taken away suddenly, and the shock of light meant he could barely make out the soldier who was now leaving the room, closing the door behind him with a loud slam.

It was a small, windowless room with a high ceiling. Fixed into an adjacent wall there was a wide mirror, and in every upper corner what looked like small cameras of some sort, mounted on brackets. Michael was sat at a table, and multicoloured wires were stuck to his chest and scalp. He could see a single, featureless grey door in the opposite wall.

His head still throbbed with pain but he could remember what had happened. The hospital, and then the jump; finding himself in a loading bay, and the men with guns.

Michael looked up at one of the cameras, and he saw it move slightly to point straight at him. Within seconds, the door opened, and two soldiers walked in, followed by a bald man in a white lab coat. The soldiers stood in each corner of the room, their guns aimed squarely at Michael's head, as the bald man approached him.

'Good morning. My name is Dr Frayn. Could you tell us your name?' he asked.

'I'm not telling you anything,' said Michael. 'Not until you tell me why you're treating me like this. Who are you?'

'Mm,' said Dr Frayn. 'British accent. Twenty, maybe twenty-five years old. All readings say human.' He huffed, and began circling the table at which Michael sat. 'EEG and heart rate picking up a certain degree of discomfort. Aggression levels low, but rising. Fear levels high. Nothing to suggest abnormal strength.'

'Who are you?' Michael shouted, but the bald man ignored him.

'Some readings picking up a low-resonance electromagnetic pulse. Awaiting tech-team evaluation. X-rays picked up a fractured rib. No irregularities in organic or genetic make-up. Blood type B. A smoker. Minor traces of alcohol present in blood stream. Cholesterol levels low.'

'Please, just tell me where I am,' said Michael, sobbing now. 'I just want to know where I am.'

'Subject shows signs of disorientation, possibly concussion. Slight bruising on left side of face, confirmed as result of blow to the head. No other injuries resulting.'

Now Frayn faced him directly, and smiled, but there was something mechanical and cold about the expression.

'Can you remember how you got here?' he asked.

'It was the crate,' said Michael, still crying. 'I work at the docks. That's all I do. I work at the docks, and there was a crate. It blew up. The others…'

He looked away from Dr Frayn to the mirror on the wall. He barely recognised himself. How long had he been travelling? How long had this been going on? Days, perhaps? And yet, to him, it felt like an eternity. Time had no meaning any more.

'Tell us your name,' said Frayn, his voice a curious mixture of interrogation and concern. 'Tell us your name, then we can help you.'

'Michael,' he replied. 'Michael Bellini.'

Dr Frayn turned to the soldiers.

'I think that's enough for now,' he said. 'Put the hood on him again, and somebody give Bev Stanley a wake-up call. This is her watch from now on.'

Michael struggled against the restraints, throwing his head from side to side, in the seconds before his world was plunged into darkness once more.

In the darkness and seclusion, it was easy to lose track of time. He tried to count the seconds and then make a mental note of the minutes, but it was no good. He could have been alone in that room for minutes, or hours. It made no difference.

When the hood was lifted again, he saw a smartly dressed woman with shoulder-length black hair and a smile that looked forced.

'Hello, Michael,' she said. 'I'm Bev Stanley. I'm the manager here at Information Retrieval. Basically, I'm just here to brief you on why we are holding you, and looking at what efforts can be made, going forward, to resolve your issue.'

What did any of these words mean? What was she talking about?

Bev Stanley sat in the chair opposite and opened a large folder out onto the table. 'Now it says here that you were found in Loading Bay 5 at around ten minutes past five last night. Is that right?'

Michael shrugged. 'I don't know,' he said. 'I was in a big room. It… It might have been that place you just said. I don't know.'

'OK,' said Bev Stanley. 'It says here you've been gone since 1967. Is that right?'

Michael stopped breathing. What was that supposed to mean? What happened in 1967?

'No?' said Bev, sensing his confusion. 'That doesn't mean anything to you? 1967?'

'How could it?' said Michael. 'What are you talking about?'

'Now, Mr Bellini, there really is no need for you to raise your voice. As I said, we are simply trying to resolve this issue. It says here that you were involved in the Hamilton's Sugar incident in 1967? I can only go by what it says in our files.'

'Well I wasn't,' said Michael.

'OK,' said Bev. 'Could you state your date of birth?'

'First of April 1929,' said Michael.

'And who is the Prime Minister?' she asked.

'Winston Churchill,' he replied. He was getting sick of being asked that question.

'And your current address?'

'Number 6, Fitzhamon Terrace, Butetown, Cardiff.'

Bev made notes and then began reading from a printed

memo. 'OK,' she said, 'I am obliged to inform you that your rights as a civilian have been withdrawn in accordance with International Security Protocol 49 and, as such, we are allowed to hold you here to assist us with our enquiries for as long as is deemed necessary. Your circumstances being as they are, you do not qualify for such terms as outlined in the European Convention on Human Rights or the 1998 Human Rights Act. While our medical team has designated you as Human, your—' she squinted at the piece of paper she had before her '—*apparent temporal displacement* renders any such rights null and void.' Still reading, she added, 'We apologise sincerely for any inconvenience this may have caused you, and hope to resolve the matter as soon as possible.'

She folded the piece of paper and returned it to the folder, offering him one more smile before she left the room.

He was alone in the room for several hours before anyone else came to see him, hours in which he had little to do but think. He struggled to remember a time before any of this started, the times when he, Hassan, Frank and Wilf would go to the Ship and Pilot after a day's work and laugh at dirty jokes, but the memories were still there. Sometimes, somebody would play the piano and they would sing, or some poor sod would have one too many and knock a table over on their way out, and the whole pub would cheer. Sometimes Wilf's wife would come into the pub, still wearing her slippers, and physically grab him by the ear and drag him home for dinner.

It had been a tough life with long hours, but he had been happy. He wasn't worried about settling down, especially not with Maggie Jenkins. What rush was there? He was happy doing what he was doing, and right now he'd have given everything he had to sit in the Ship and Pilot and hear his friends sing.

Now he wondered whether he was still alive. At first, everything had seemed like a dream, or rather a nightmare, but now, now that he knew this *wasn't* a dream, it felt like death, or how he imagined death might feel. Was this Hell?

He hadn't been to Confession in a long time; at least since his father died. Was this his punishment? All the sinful thoughts he'd had, all the times he'd sworn, the times he'd been angry with God as he saw his father sink into the bottom of a bottle of Bells, or when his Aunty Megan had told him that his mother was in Heaven now. When life had stopped making so much sense he'd forgotten about church altogether. Was this his sentence?

Perhaps he hadn't survived the explosion. Perhaps, like the others, he had been killed, and this was a Hell designed especially for him. A Hell in which everyone was cruel and uncaring and spoke nonsense, and demons with bowler hats terrorised young children. It even crossed his mind that he might spend eternity in that room, no longer than ten feet and no wider than six – an eternity strapped into a chair, alone.

One thing he knew for sure, if there was any chance of getting out of this barren, soulless place, was that he was tired of running. He'd tired, already, of being afraid, and of running away from things he didn't understand. If he could only get out of this chair and this room he was going to fight back. He was going to find out all about Torchwood, and about the men in bowler hats, and he was going to fight them with every drop of strength he could muster.

His thoughts were interrupted, suddenly, by the opening of the door, and the appearance of a man he recognised, only now he was so much older.

Cromwell.

'Michael,' he said, shuffling into the room, bracing himself against his walking stick. 'Michael Michael Michael… It's been so many years.'

A uniformed guard entered the room, pulling out the spare chair, and Cromwell sat down.

'Old legs not as strong as they used to be,' he said, smiling softly. 'And no space on the helicopter to stretch them, either. Bumpy ride too, choppers. Never liked them. Like sitting inside a cocktail shaker. It was so much better when you could catch the train.'

He sighed, and took off his trilby, dabbing at his now-crinkled forehead with a handkerchief.

'Michael,' he said, smiling, 'I'd begun to think we wouldn't see you again. You've been quite the will-o'-the-wisp for us, really you have. We almost caught up with you a few years back, in Cardiff, so I'm told. They sent somebody to the hospital where they were keeping you, but then you were gone. Done a Houdini. Strapped into a bed, and yet somehow you vanished like a puff of smoke.

Most impressive. How long ago *was* that, now?'

'It was yesterday,' said Michael.

Cromwell paused, looking Michael in the eye, and then burst into laughter.

'Yesterday?' he said. 'Oh yes, I suppose it *feels* like yesterday, and perhaps for you it *was* yesterday, but for us? Oh, Michael… I wish there were a single one of us who could understand what has happened to you. It's been quite a curious few years, on and off. I really thought we'd seen the last of you in '67, but here you are…'

'Sixty-seven?' said Michael. 'They keep mentioning 1967 but I don't know what they're talking about.'

'No,' said Cromwell, 'I don't suppose you would. To us everything has been moving in a straight line, but for you…' He shook his head and raised his hands in resignation. 'For you it's like a Chinese puzzle, is it not? Popping up, here and there: 1967, your arrest, the training hospital a few years back. Can you even remember half of these things? I doubt it. Oh, Michael, if only we could have had the chance to study you. If only we'd known, those first few days after the explosion. If only we'd had the laws we have nowadays. It was much harder to simply have someone disappear off the streets in '53.'

Cromwell laughed, and once again mopped his brow, chuckling softly.

'So long ago now,' he said. 'For me, at least. You, on the other hand, haven't aged a bit. It must seem like days, to you. There was a boy out there, on reception, probably about your age. Funny boy. Sounded like he was from our side of the bridge, somewhere up in the valleys, I reckon. Stuttered and spluttered his way around asking me if I'd like a cup of tea. Funny to think he's young enough to be your grandson, isn't it?'

Cromwell looked across at the mirror, and ran one hand over his bald head. Michael followed his gaze. It was only now he could appreciate just what Cromwell was talking about. The last time they had met, there had been no more than ten or fifteen years between them, but now Cromwell was a very old man, and Michael was still little more than a boy.

'But time is the decider of every man's fate, is it not?' said Cromwell. 'Some of us die young, and some of us live to be very old men with weak bladders and knees that crack when we get up too quickly. Do you know how you can end this, Michael?'

And now Cromwell turned from his own reflection to look at Michael directly.

'How?' asked Michael.

'The only way,' said Cromwell, 'that this will ever end is when you die.'

'No,' said Michael, looking down to the floor, wishing he could raise his hands to cover his face. 'No, that's just another lie. Like when you came to the hospital, and you said you were from the Union… That's just another lie.'

Cromwell shook his head. 'I'm afraid it isn't, Michael. They want you, you know.'

'Who? Who wants me?'

'Somebody later told me they are called the Vondrax.

Strangest things. Some of the victims bled to death, haemorrhaging on a massive scale. Others were burnt to cinders. The sightings, the records, '67... We spent so many years piecing it together for our report, and that's when we came to the conclusion. They're after you. You're the only one who can end this.'

'No,' said Michael. 'How can I end this? What am I supposed to do?'

Cromwell was staring at him gravely when they both heard the alarm.

'Ah,' said Cromwell, 'here they are. As I thought.'

'Who?' asked Michael.

'The Vondrax,' Cromwell replied. 'It was only a matter of time.'

The door to the interview room opened, and two of the armed guards came in.

'Mr Cromwell, Miss Stanley has asked that you stay here with our visitor. It appears we have a Code 200 situation on one of the lower floors.'

'Men in bowler hats, no doubt,' said Cromwell. He seemed unnervingly at ease, as if he had experienced this too many times before.

'Y-yes, sir,' said one of the guards. 'How did you know?'

'Ask our *young* friend, here,' said Cromwell, smiling broadly. 'He is an *old* friend of theirs.'

The guards looked from Cromwell to Michael and back again.

'I didn't mean literally,' said Cromwell. 'It was a figure of speech.'

The guards left the room and the door closed. Michael pulled against his restraints, but it was no good.

'Trying to escape?' said Cromwell. 'There really is no need, you know. You're always best at escaping when you aren't even trying.'

'But we need to get out of here!'

'Me, perhaps, yes,' said Cromwell. 'There's every chance I won't be getting out of this one in any fighting condition, but you… You're what they call a dead cert.'

'What do you mean?'

Cromwell didn't answer him, he simply looked at his watch. Somewhere in the building there was an explosion. Even inside a room that was apparently soundproof, it could be heard, and more than heard – it could be *felt*.

'Here they come,' said Cromwell. 'Like children of the cosmos, I've always felt. So much chaos, so much destruction, so much pointless cruelty, and all they want is their ball back.'

'You're talking in riddles!' shouted Michael. 'Get me out of this chair. You're insane!'

'Oh no,' said Cromwell. 'After fifty odd years of this I am finally quite sane. There's nothing like knowing the future, or in this case the past, to put your mind at ease.'

He looked at Michael, his expression suddenly warm and compassionate, filled with feeling.

'I never did apologise for what we did to you,' he said, smiling softly. 'I never said sorry.'

He closed his eyes serenely, as if he were listening to some soothing piano sonata and, as he did so, the mirror in the wall shattered, sending shards of two-way glass tumbling to the ground.

'They're getting closer,' said Cromwell, his eyes still shut, his expression beatific. 'They don't like mirrors.'

The sound of another explosion, louder now that the two-way mirror was broken, and Michael could see through into the darkened, adjoining room. He could hear people screaming, somewhere beyond the observation room, and in the darkness he saw moving, shadowy forms.

'Please,' said Michael, 'just get me out of this chair. We need to get out of here, now…'

'You don't,' said Cromwell. '*You'll* be just fine.'

The shapes in the darkness were becoming steadily more visible as each one came into the light from the interrogation room. They looked like men, at first, but then they always did. As each one was illuminated, an identical face was revealed, that same, grey-skinned sneering face, its eyes hidden behind round, black sunglasses, the leering mouth opening to reveal sharply pointed teeth.

'The Traveller…' they said as one.

Cromwell opened his eyes, and looked through the broken mirror as the Vondrax drew nearer. All at once they stopped, each of them breathing heavily, a foul hissing that emanated from their throats, their talon-like fingers wrapped around the jagged, gaping wound in the wall where the mirror had been, poised to enter the interrogation room.

Cromwell turned to face Michael and saw nothing but an empty chair.

'Clever boy,' he said, laughing to himself.

He turned back to face the shattered mirror, and looked straight into the eyes of the Vondrax.

ELEVEN

The opening chords of T-Rex's '20th Century Boy' blasted into his ears as Jack Harkness walked down Carnaby Street on a late summer's morning in 1967. Never mind that the song would not be recorded for another six years, or that the device on which he was listening to it, the C-Fish X20, would not be invented for another six decades. Anachronisms weren't important to Jack, and the earphones were practically invisible so it wasn't as if anyone might notice. What mattered was that the song seemed *right*.

The C-Fish, a portable music player, had, along with the contents of his bag, been deposited in a locker at King's Cross by Jack himself a long time and many lives ago, back in the days when time was no barrier. He'd thought that both might come in handy one day, and he was right.

Looking around at the assorted mods and hippies – girls in fluorescent miniskirts, Union Flag-patterned waistcoats and baker-boy caps; men in flared jeans and paisley shirts made of cheesecloth – it struck Jack that immortality, rather than rendering life predictable, often made it even more surprising. A life stretched out for more than a century made changes that had happened quite gradually to the casual observer, seem sudden and revolutionary.

Only a few years ago, on his last visit, he had walked down this street to find it populated by austere tailors and nattily dressed jazz musicians looking for just the right threads. Now it was an explosion of garish, psychedelic colour, with music blaring from the open doors of almost every shop.

He wasn't simply there as a tourist or even an observer, however. Jack had a purpose that morning. There were questions to be answered. Somebody in London had been asking questions about Jack Harkness, and Jack was going to find out who.

He'd been in the city little more than three hours, but already he could sense that people were on to him. A car had tailed him across much of the city, a black Rover P6, driven by a man in a grey cap. Amateurs, Jack had thought. Whoever they were, travelling incognito was clearly not their forte. Still, for now he was in the clear. The streets of Soho were a good place to lose anyone who might be following you; a labyrinthine network of interconnecting thoroughfares and alleyways boxed in by the busy, traffic-congested arteries of Shaftsbury Avenue, Oxford Street and Charing Cross Road. Here was a village within the city; a chaotic heart, beating to a syncopated rhythm, in the very centre of the metropolis.

His destination was a restaurant on Golden Square called Houghton's. In the vibrant, noisy kaleidoscope of Soho, it was an oasis of gentlemanly calm, a throwback to a bygone era. It was also the place where he would meet Hugo.

Hugo Faulkner was the third son of Baron Faulkner of Darrington, and was every bit the third son of a peer of the realm. While his older brothers had enjoyed illustrious military careers and were now major players in the City, Hugo was something of a black sheep; the decadent man about town, renowned for his lavish parties and almost bohemian lifestyle. He traded in antiquities and fine art, an almost respectable profession to any family except the Faulkners, who measured a man's worth in medals.

The restaurant itself had the feeling of an Edwardian time capsule: burgundy velvet and real Tiffany lampshades; a fog of cigar smoke clouding the ceiling, and a soundtrack of clinking cutlery and bullish voices. It was jarring to Jack, who had eaten in such places when they were the norm, rather than the exception, as if he had inadvertently stumbled into his own past. On his arrival at the restaurant, he was taken by the maître d' to a table in the far corner, where Hugo Faulkner was already waiting for him.

Jack was surprised by his appearance. The man's reputation had suggested something far less dapper. He'd expected long hair, a beard perhaps, and appropriated ethnic clothing, but was greeted instead by a very tall young man with foppish blond hair, dressed in a pinstripe suit and pink tie.

'Mr Faulkner?' said Jack.

Hugo stood, holding out his hand. 'Hugo, please. You must be Mr Williamson?'

'Tim.'

'Tim… Very pleased to meet you.' He shook Jack's hand with a weak grip and sat down again. 'Would you care for tea? Or coffee? Perhaps something stronger? They have a splendid 1948 Colheita, if you're a port-drinking man.'

'I'm fine,' said Jack. He was already opening the bag that he had carried through Soho, and lifting a small wooden box from inside.

Hugo's eyes lit up and he gasped with delight. 'Is that it?'

Jack nodded.

'This is it,' he said, placing the box on the table and opening it gently. Inside, wrapped in linen, was a thick, yellowing manuscript, dog-eared around its edges. The title page read:

Cardenio – A Spanish Comedie
by Messrs William Shaksper and John Fletcher

'My God…' said Hugo, reaching for it with both hands.

'Easy, tiger,' said Jack. 'It's over three hundred and fifty years old. Here, I've brought gloves.'

Jack handed him a pair of white cotton gloves. Hugo put them on and began delicately turning the pages.

'Yes yes,' he said. 'The handwriting certainly resembles Shakespeare's. Some of it… here for example… that's clearly Fletcher's work, but this… this is Shakespeare.'

'Impressed?' said Jack.

146

'Yes, I'm very impressed. If it's not too vulgar for me to jump to the matter of remuneration, how much were you asking? For the manuscript?'

'Three thousand,' said Jack, bluntly. 'Is that too much?'

Hugo laughed. 'Oh, I shouldn't think so,' he said. 'I've never been able to understand why it is some people struggle for money when there's so much of the stuff floating about. You simply need to know how to catch it, most of the time. Like collecting butterflies. Would you mind if I write it as a cheque? I don't tend to carry much cash around. Dirtiest thing you can touch, cash. All those hands, all their germs. Makes you shudder just to think about it.'

'A cheque's fine,' said Jack.

'OK,' said Hugo, producing a Coutt's chequebook and a fountain pen. 'Who should I make this out to? Timothy Williamson?'

'Yes,' said Jack, still forcing a smile.

'Or perhaps Jack Harkness?' said Hugo, and Jack's smile faded.

'What did you say?' he asked.

'Really,' said Hugo, continuing as if he hadn't said a thing, 'this is a remarkable find. Scholars have been arguing over *Cardenio* for centuries, and we'd quite safely assumed it was lost for eternity. Why *should* a reasonably obscure work survive so many floods, fires, and bombs? Why, if it were not that notable a play, should posterity have saved it? And yet here it is. Remarkable.'

'What did you say?' Jack asked again, more forcefully this time.

'I said it's remarkable that the play should have survived. Although I'm particularly curious because I happen to know that there was a surviving copy of *Cardenio* in London as recently as 1765, but that it was stolen from the home of Thomas Sheridan by a man claiming, rather ludicrously, to be a *time agent*. A man by the name of Jack Harkness.'

Jack paused. Had his moment's caution been premature? Was it just Hugo's idea of a joke to call him by that name?

'Fancy that!' said Hugo. 'A *time* agent. Of all the things… Of course, Sheridan's words remained in private correspondence that I was lucky enough to come across a few years back. A secret auction in Bloomsbury. Sheridan thought this Harkness fellow to be a scoundrel and a liar, and so didn't believe a word the man said, but the fact remains, the manuscript *was* stolen.'

'I see,' said Jack. 'Well, I don't know anything about that. I just bought this from a friend. More of an acquaintance, really.'

'I see,' said Hugo. 'Although, the strangest thing is that Sheridan's description of his visitor bears an uncanny resemblance to you. The description is quite exact, right down to the accent. Of course, he described it as "colonial", and not "American", as we might today.'

Jack began to laugh. 'Hugo,' he said, 'you really are something else. Honestly, man, I can't keep up with that surreal English sense of humour of yours. Time Agents? 1765? Thomas Sheridan?'

'Oh, please, Jack, cut the pantomime. I think we both know what I'm talking about. Or rather, you know a little more than I do, but I'm on the right track, aren't I? Did you think that you were the spider and I was the fly?'

Jack scowled at him, and Hugo roared with laughter.

'Oh, Jack, that really is quite endearing of you. You thought that *you* had come here to ensnare *me*? Oh, you may very well have been the one who contacted me, but didn't you think it was all just a little too easy?'

'Who are you?' Jack asked, his tone harder now, any last traces of pretence having washed away.

'*I* am who I say I am,' said Hugo. 'I'm Hugo Faulkner, son of Baron Faulkner of Darrington and celebrated bon vivant. I have the papers to prove it.' He slowly removed the white cotton gloves. 'The question is, Jack, who are you?'

'Who do you work for?' asked Jack. He was breathing heavily, barely able to contain his anger. How had this situation turned so quickly? He had come here to ask the questions, not to be interrogated himself.

'I am part of an organisation that asks questions,' said Hugo. 'And sometimes we provide answers. There is a cancer, Jack, at the heart of this country. Secrets and lies which threaten to destabilise everything. The days of Empire are behind us, and Britain is far from great. My organisation plans to capitalise on that. You might be interested in joining us, Jack.'

'I'm not.'

Hugo frowned, mockingly, with a childish pout.

'Oh, really, Jack? So dismissive? With nary a second thought? That's a shame. I'd hoped you'd see things differently.'

'Well I really have to be going,' said Jack, flashing Hugo an empty smile. 'Maybe I'll see you around.'

'Oh, I do hope so,' said Hugo. 'That would be wonderful.'

Jack stood but, as he turned to leave, Hugo reached out and grabbed him by the sleeve of his coat.

'Jack… You forgot your gloves.'

As he left the restaurant, his heart racing, Jack saw it again: the Rover P6, parked in the shadow of a tree in one corner of Golden Square. The driver was reading the *Daily Telegraph*, but the newspaper was lowered just an inch or two, and Jack saw the driver staring straight at him. Across the street from the parked car, two more men appeared to be having a conversation, but one of the men looked at him and held his gaze just a second longer than he should.

Jack left the square and walked down Brewer Street. Looking back just once, he saw the man in the Rover signal to the two men who had been talking, and very suddenly he was being followed.

Jack's pace quickened and he crossed the street to escape their field of view. As he reached the junction with Lexington Street, he ran into a small army of Hare Krishnas, perhaps fifty of them in all, dancing and singing and beating tambourines. He weaved his way through the sea of saffron-coloured robes and the din of the music, and joked to himself that this was one occasion when karma had come to the rescue.

Once he had freed himself from the musical throng, Jack began to run. Running wasn't really his style, or at least not running *away*, but he did so out of necessity. Something had gone very wrong with his plan. He'd intended to ask questions, and he supposed he'd gotten answers, but he'd never expected them to be waiting for him like that. He had to get back to Cardiff, and quickly.

First things first, though. The Hare Krishnas had provided a much-needed distraction but the two men were still chasing him. He ran as far as Dean Street, the men closing in on him, until he came to the narrow alleyway where he'd left his British racing green Triumph GT6.

Leaping into the car, he turned the key in the ignition, and the modified V8 engine roared into life. Jack was about to hit the accelerator when two pursuers appeared at the far end of the alleyway.

Slowly, they made their way towards him, their smug grins telling him they thought they had him cornered. Jack revved the engine once, twice, and spotted a moment's hesitation in their eyes in the split second before he put his foot down and drove straight for them.

One man leapt out of the way, crashing into the piles of old wooden crates and cardboard boxes that lined the alleyway, but the second was not so lucky. He was glanced by the front left wing, and sent spinning in the air like a rag doll, crashing face first onto the tarmac.

Jack hurtled along Dean Street before swerving sharply out into Oxford Street, barely missing the front of a red double-decker bus and the back end of a taxi. Horns blared and people gasped, and the engine of the Triumph growled furiously over the din.

Jack was clear. Almost. He was on the junction with Regent Street when the Rover from Golden Square veered out into the centre of the thoroughfare, its wheels hissing and screaming against tarmac, and began to give chase.

With its polished chrome bumper kissing the taillights of the Triumph, the Rover followed Jack as he weaved in and out of the traffic, tearing through red light after red light, swerving left and right. They drew nearer to the junction at Marble Arch, and all Jack could see ahead were streams of traffic in both directions.

He looked up at the rear-view mirror, and saw the steely glare of the Rover's driver; he betrayed no intention of slowing down. This was it; another dance with death.

In one sudden move, Jack pulled back the handbrake, sending the Triumph into a sharp spin. He was now facing the oncoming traffic, but clear of the path of the Rover, which skidded out into an onslaught of vehicles on Park Lane. It was smashed in one direction and then another by two buses, resting finally, a battered wreck, in the centre of the road. Broken and bloody, the driver's body lay hunched over the steering wheel, pressing down on the horn, which let out an unending wail.

Jack reversed, and then turned, driving past the steaming hulk, now barely recognisable as a car, before hitting the accelerator once more. He barely slowed down for the whole of his journey out of the city. He would glance, occasionally, at the rear-view mirror, but nobody was tailing him. Not now. They presumably had better sense.

He was on the great grey runway of the Severn Bridge while, on the radio, Jimi Hendrix sang about being 'Stone Free' when it happened.

First the music was drowned out by an agitated crackling. Then the interior of the car became a little warmer. There was a sound like the banging of an enormous drum, and suddenly Jack was not alone.

Sat beside him was a young man in shabby grey clothes; a boy maybe twenty or twenty-five years old, with black hair and blue eyes.

'Oh God…' said the boy, as if in abject terror. 'Oh my God… Jack?'

The car swerved, first left, then right, and then span 360 degrees before Jack hit the brakes and brought it screeching to a halt.

'What the…'

'Jack?'

'Who are you?'

'It's me,' said the boy. 'Don't you know me?

For a moment, Jack simply sat in silence. Glancing up at the mirror, he saw an articulated truck coming up behind them, so he started the engine again and carried on driving.

'What are you doing in my car?' he said, eventually. 'I mean… How did you… Who… How… No… *What are you doing in my car?*'

'Don't you know me?' Michael asked. 'It's Michael. We met. You know me.'

'No,' he said. 'That's not possible. Who are you?'

'I'm Michael,' said the boy.

Jack had never seen anybody eat so quickly or with so much enthusiasm. They were in a Chinese café in the centre of Cardiff, away from the windows but close enough to a door should they need to make a quick getaway. It was the way Jack always did things.

The boy, Michael, had tried to tell him several things; about the place in the future where they had met, about the things that had happened there, but Jack had stopped him. The slightest wrong word and everything could be thrown out of balance. Besides, who *really* wanted to know their future, from beginning to end? The sort of thing most people wanted to know was winning horses. They would much prefer to leave the rest to fate, destiny and chance. He'd stuck to this rule, and he'd followed it more closely than he could have ever imagined back in the days when he'd played by a very relaxed set of rules. A year ago, he hadn't even placed any bets on England winning the World Cup, and he could have really cleaned up on *that* occasion.

'You enjoying that?' Jack said, pointing at the near-empty plate.

Michael nodded. 'I've never eaten Chinese food before,' he said. 'What are these?' He held up his fork.

'That's a bean sprout,' said Jack, laughing.

'Oh,' said Michael. 'They looked horrible at first but they're quite nice. I haven't eaten a thing in ages. Not since… Actually, I can't remember the last time I ate. Not properly, anyway. There were these things, like peas in the pod, in Japan, but other than that, nothing.'

'Mm…' said Jack. 'You should think about marketing that. The Time Traveller's Diet. Lose weight in no time.'

Michael frowned, not really understanding what Jack was talking about, and resumed eating.

'Look, Michael…' said Jack. 'I understand that things must be a little crazy for you, but…'

He trailed off. Michael had dropped food onto his shirt and was frantically dabbing at it with a napkin, while occasionally glancing up at Jack in embarrassment.

'Sorry,' he said. 'I just… I don't normally eat like this.'

'It's OK,' said Jack. 'You were hungry.'

'What were you going to say?'

'When?'

'Just now. You said things must be crazy for me, and then you stopped talking.'

'Nothing,' said Jack. 'It's nothing.'

'You still didn't answer my question,' said Michael, before shovelling another forkful of food into his mouth.

'And which question was that?' asked Jack.

'How? How come you don't get any older?'

Jack sighed. 'It's not that I don't get any older,' he said. 'I do. Everyone gets older. I just do it a little slower than most people.'

'But how?'

'I don't know,' said Jack. 'I'm waiting for an answer, but I guess I've got a lot more waiting to do.'

'You sound sad,' said Michael. 'I thought nobody wanted to get old.'

'Like I told you,' said Jack, 'everyone gets old.'

As Michael scooped up the last remaining morsels from his plate their waitress came to the table, handing Jack a note. Jack opened it and read:

Jack,
No reason to be afraid, old chap. I may be able to help you
out with your concerns. If you really are looking for answers
I'd suggest you turn up at the fairground, Barry Island, 9pm
sharp tomorrow.
Ciao.

'From the gentleman across the street, sir. He said he wanted you to read it…?'

The waitress pointed through a window on the other side of the café, and looking across the street Jack saw a man standing beneath the awning of a neighbouring restaurant.

It was Hugo.

TWELVE

'Well what time *will* you be coming home?' Rhys's voice was tinny and vaguely crackling at the other end of the phone line. Another thing they needed to put on the wedding list: a new phone.

'I don't know, love,' said Gwen. 'Like I said, something's come up at the last minute. I won't be here much longer, I promise.'

'I cooked you tea and everything,' said Rhys. 'Spaghetti bolognese. I even bought that cheese you like.'

Ah, spaghetti bolognese, thought Gwen. Rhys's current, culinary way of saying sorry. She was tired of it now, of course, after so many apologies that had sent him running to the kitchen after a quick jaunt to the nearest supermarket. Spag bol, as he called it, and a bottle of the supermarket's best own-brand red wine. Even though she hadn't gone to the supermarket with him, she could so easily imagine him pulling faces at anything that cost more than a fiver.

'We'll eat when I get home,' said Gwen.

'But what time's that going to be?' asked Rhys. 'I'm bloody starving *now*, and it's gone ten o'clock. I got work in the morning.'

He was right, of course. He may have been the one cooking spaghetti bolognese, but why should he have to wait for her until midnight or later? Gwen sighed.

Across the Hub, Owen was reading through a backlog of archive materials relating to the 1953 explosion and to the investigation which had followed it. He signalled to Gwen several times, waving his hand in the air, but Gwen shook her head.

'I'm sorry, Rhys,' she said into the phone. 'I've got to go, seriously. I won't be long, love, I promise.'

She said goodbye to him, and then the line went dead.

'What is it?' she called to Owen. 'What is it that so *desperately* needed my attention?'

'Look at this,' said Owen, pointing at his screen. 'I've managed to find something on the Orb investigation. But that's not all.'

'What is it?' asked Gwen, crossing the Hub and looking down at his monitor.

'Here,' said Owen, tapping the screen. 'Says the investigation into the explosion failed to find a cause, though it was believed… God, I think I need to get glasses or something, or is the print just really small? It was believed that Rift energy could not be ruled out as a factor. Jack was right. Then it says nothing happened at Torchwood Cardiff for another fourteen years, when "key personnel"… who the bloody hell are *key personnel*? Anyway… *Key personnel*…

investigated the "Hamilton's Sugar incident".'

'And that was?'

'Your guess is as good as mine. I've searched everything on our database. I've gone through everything we salvaged from Torchwood One. Nothing. Not a sausage. That's the last information I can find relating to Michael. The trail goes cold, and it wasn't particularly hot to begin with.'

Owen got up from his workstation.

'Anyway,' he said, 'I'm going to the Boardroom to keep an eye on Michael. I've got a really bad feeling…'

'What about?' asked Gwen.

'I don't know,' said Owen. 'But I have.'

Toshiko stared at the Orb. She'd listened to everything Jack had said, but even now it made little or no sense. In her time with Torchwood, she had grown accustomed to so many strange and inexplicable things. She had seen spaceships and aliens and she had travelled in time, but this was different.

It was her nightmares. She realised that had something to do with it. Listening to Jack talk about the Vondrax, and to the others describing what they had seen and heard… It was as if her worst childhood fears had been proven to exist. The monster under the bed was no longer a dark fantasy explained away by an infant's overactive imagination; it was real.

The Orb itself was now quite dead. The readings she had picked up earlier seemed to diminish by the minute, leaving just the metal husk. The first metallurgy tests she had been able to perform confirmed one further, perplexing detail. Whatever metal the ball was made from could be found nowhere on the periodic table. It shared properties with titanium and zinc, without being identifiable as either. Though it appeared to be quite hollow, with a crust no more than a centimetre thick, it weighed in excess of forty kilos.

The engravings on its surface looked like ancient hieroglyphs but, from the little she knew of Egyptian, Sumerian and other writing forms, it had nothing in common with anything from Earth. Why should it? If Jack was to be believed, this thing was probably older than the Earth itself.

And then there was Michael. *Poor Michael*, as she had taken to thinking of him. It was clear to her now that the Michael asleep in the Boardroom had never met her, that their experiences in Osaka had not yet happened to him. Where would this end for him, she wondered? She felt so redundant and helpless. Why wasn't there anything she could do for him? With all the technology they had at their disposal, they were still able to do nothing more than observe.

It was as she drew sketches of some of the engravings on the surface of the Orb that Toshiko saw it. In the corner of her eye, on one of her monitors, a shape moved out of the shadows in Basement D-4. She turned her head quickly to look at it, and was sure she saw it clearly, if only for a split second.

The silhouette of a man wearing a bowler hat.

No sooner was she facing the monitor than the shadowy form had vanished. She took in a deep shuddering breath and quickly checked the motion sensors within the vault. There was nothing there.

There was nothing left for him to do, as a doctor. He'd carried out every necessary test, written every report that needed to be written. The professional part of his role had been satisfied, and now he was just here, in the Boardroom, with the patient. With Michael.

Michael was sleeping a little more easily now, curled up on one side in a foetal position, breathing quietly, his eyes resting beneath his eyelids.

'You're going to be OK,' Owen said. At first he felt ridiculous talking to someone who was asleep. It was something you did with people in comas, of course, but not somebody who was simply sleeping.

'I wish there was more we could do for you, mate, really I do. It's just that sometimes we don't have the answers. Oh, of course, Jack knows a lot, but not *everything*. I'm not sure we'll ever be able to stop this from happening to you. I mean… *tachyon radiation*. I'd never even bloody heard of it until an hour ago. And those things… the Vondrax… If they came for you before I guess they'll be coming for you again.'

He took a deep breath.

'But don't worry, mate,' he said. 'This time we'll be waiting for them.'

Jack didn't hear Ianto enter the office. He didn't even know he was there until he felt a hand on his shoulder and heard his voice.

'Are you OK?'

'Yeah,' said Jack, putting his hand over Ianto's and squeezing it gently. 'Yeah, I'm fine.'

There was a moment's silence before Ianto spoke again.

'It's been a funny evening, hasn't it?' he said.

Jack frowned.

'Funny?' he said. 'Funny how? Funny ha, ha or funny peculiar?'

'Oh,' said Ianto, 'funny peculiar. Definitely funny peculiar. Well, it's not two hours since I had my feet up and was watching *Goldfinger*. It's felt like a long night.'

'Every night's long,' said Jack.

'Are you being enigmatic with me?' asked Ianto. 'You know most of it goes over my head. I'd have to wade through the collected works of Sartre before I could properly get inside that skull of yours.'

'Am I *that* enigmatic?' asked Jack.

'Sometimes,' said Ianto.

There was near silence again, but for the soft humming of machines.

'Should I be jealous?' Ianto asked.

Jack span around in his chair.

'What do you mean?'

Ianto pointed at Jack's monitor, where Jack had been watching an image of Michael sleeping.

'What?' Jack asked. 'What are you talking about?'

'We've all met him before,' said Ianto. 'Before we came here. You said yourself that you knew him before tonight.'

'And I *did*.'

'How well?'

Jack said nothing.

'If there's anything you need to do,' said Ianto, 'you should just do it. I don't *own* you. I can't *stop* you.'

Jack looked up at Ianto and smiled weakly.

'It's not as easy as that, is it?' he said. 'The kid who's sleeping in the Boardroom doesn't know me. He doesn't know what happens next. That's *my* past and *his* future. I can't say anything to him. I can't *stop* it from happening.'

'You can't stop what from happening?' asked Ianto. 'What happened?'

THIRTEEN

'I look stupid,' said Michael, standing before the full-length mirror in the hotel room, wearing a pair of purple corduroy trousers, a brown cheesecloth shirt and a purple waistcoat.

'You don't look stupid,' said Jack. 'A little eccentric, perhaps, but no more eccentric than anyone else out there. This *is* the Sixties. You can't go round in those utility clothes of yours. Besides, it's not like you paid for them.'

Michael looked at Jack and smiled. 'Thanks,' he said.

The hotel was nothing special; in fact, Jack might even go as far as to say it was sub par, but he'd stayed in worse places and, for the time being, Michael would be safe here.

It was a ramshackle place near the town, sandwiched between a turf accountant and a dilapidated Victorian theatre. The sign at the front said 'The Sh ngri La Hot l', but it was as far removed from James Hilton's fictional paradise as could be imagined. At least, Jack supposed, its low-rent nature and lack of luxury meant the owner, a woman with a tattoo of a rose on her hand and an addiction to crosswords, was unlikely to ask too many questions. Many strange things had no doubt happened at the Shangri-La Hotel.

The room was basic, with just a double bed, a small desk and a chair. The curtains were orange nylon, and the bathroom was in the corridor and shared by eight other rooms. Michael didn't seem to mind. He'd never stayed in a hotel before.

'You say you've got a sister?' Jack asked.

'Yeah,' said Michael. 'She lives in Butetown. At least, I think she does.'

'Do you think she'd still live there?'

Michael shrugged.

'Well,' said Jack, 'it's got to be worth a try, hasn't it?'

He didn't want to tell Michael that this was his plan. They would find Michael's sister, and then Michael would be free, free from forces he'd never understand, and Jack would be able to deal with the issue of Hugo.

'Can you remember where she lives?' asked Jack.

'Yeah,' said Michael. 'Number 6, Fitzhamon Terrace. I lived there. It was like yesterday. It *was* yesterday…'

'Well, she's as good a place to start as any,' said Jack.

Michael nodded, but Jack could tell that something was troubling him. He hardly spoke again until they were driving through the city's streets towards Butetown.

'Everything's changing,' said Michael, looking out through the window. 'Every time I'm here something's different. Something's changed.'

'It's the way of the world, kiddo,' said Jack. 'No point trying to fight time.'

Michael nodded dolefully, but he still couldn't take it in. This place, this city, was meant to be his home, and yet it couldn't have seemed more alien, more different to him. There were buildings he knew, of course, but so many that he didn't. Some buildings that he had expected to see were no longer there; whole streets razed to the ground, leaving nothing but wide open wasteland filled with nothing but gravel and weeds. He wondered, sadly, whether he'd ever see his real home; the home he really knew, again.

They reached Fitzhamon Terrace, and Jack parked up alongside the house.

'This is it,' said Michael. 'Number 6. I live… She lives here. At least I hope she still does.'

'Well go on, then,' said Jack, gesturing towards the door. 'What are you waiting for?'

Michael nodded and got out of the car. He climbed the steps to the front door, rapped the knocker several times, and then waited. From inside the house, he heard the sound of a dog barking, and then quick footsteps on a staircase.

The door was opened by a teenager with floppy hair and an adolescent attempt at a moustache.

'Hello?' said the boy, in a flat and inexpressive monotone.

'Hello,' said Michael. 'Does Maria Bellini, I mean James, Maria James… Does she live here?'

The teenage boy nodded, and turned to face the other end of the house.

'Mu-um! There's someone here to see you!'

From somewhere deep inside the house, Michael heard his sister's voice. He recognised it instantly, even if time had aged it a little.

'Well who is it? If it's one of them door-to-door people, tell them I'm not interested.'

'I'm not,' said Michael, smiling at his nephew. 'Tell her it's her brother.'

The boy frowned, as if Michael had said something which couldn't possibly be true, and then, without conviction, shouted, 'He says he's your brother.'

In the dim light of the hallway, Michael saw a figure emerge from the kitchen, wearing an apron and Marigold rubber gloves. She was older than he could ever have imagined, streaks of grey in hair that had once been as black as his, crow's feet around her blue eyes, laughter lines around her mouth, but he still knew her.

'Maria…' he said. No other words came. His eyes burned, and he felt himself smile, properly smile, for the first time since as far back as he could remember. It was as if his heart couldn't be contained, as if he wanted to breathe in until he burst, as if every prayer he'd ever made had been answered in one.

Maybe now it could end, maybe now this thing would stop, and he could be safe, and home.

'Robert, go to your room,' said his sister to her son, to the boy Michael had last seen as a baby, only days before.

The boy shrugged and walked back into the house, and Michael realised that Maria wasn't smiling back at him.

'You're not my brother,' she said, shaking her head. 'My brother's dead. Years ago. Look at you. How old are you? He'd be almost forty now. You aren't Michael. How *dare* you come here and say a thing like that. Who are you? How do you know his name? How do you know where I live?'

'No…' said Michael, stepping closer to the door.

'You keep away from me, or I swear to God I will phone the police. Who are you?'

'I've told you,' said Michael. 'It's me. It's Michael. I'm back. I'm here, and I'm back, and I just wanted to—'

'Is this some kind of sick joke?' said his sister. 'My brother was missing for years. Probably drowned himself, they said. Probably jumped off a boat and drowned himself. How *dare* you come here and say these things. How *dare* you.'

She covered her mouth, and then wiped away the tears from her eyes.

'You're lucky my husband's at work,' she said. 'If he wasn't…'

'Please, Maria…' said Michael. 'I just—'

'I don't want to see you round here again,' said his sister. 'Do you hear me? I never want to see you again.'

The door closed, not with a slam but with a dull thud, and Michael was sure he could hear her sobbing on the other side. He leaned against the door, and tried to say something, anything, but he couldn't. It was pointless.

They sat in silence for the rest of the journey back to the hotel. Jack had pinned everything on the boy's sister welcoming him back with open arms, but then fourteen years was a long time. There was no textbook on how to react to a surprise like that, especially one which defied all logic. There was nothing Jack could say to console Michael; at least there was nothing he could think of, nothing that would mean anything to him. The only thing he could do was keep him safe.

Jack often liked to think that years spent waiting fruitlessly – years exposed to every grubby facet of life – had hardened him to the world, leaving him cynical enough to cope with whatever came next, and emotionally tough enough to walk away from any situation, but he knew this wasn't true. The last embers of his empathy and altruism had not yet died out completely. But what to do with Michael?

'What are we going to do?' Michael asked him, when they were back in the hotel room. The fading light of a setting sun filtered through the closed curtains, turning the whole room a fiery orange.

'In the long term, I don't know,' said Jack. 'I've got questions of my own I need answering, and you… Well, you are just one great big bundle of questions. There's a thing, tomorrow… I might have to meet up with some people. It might be nothing. Until then, I don't know. I'm fresh out of plans. But tonight… Tonight I say we go out and we drink. I mean, there's no real point in me drinking, cos I can't seem to get drunk these days, but we can sit in some noisy crowded pub somewhere and pretend that we're having a good time. Sound good to you, kiddo?'

Michael smiled. It wasn't a plan, as such, but it was better, he figured, than staying in this lifeless room and thinking about the events of the day so far. Besides which, just being with Jack made him feel safe.

The pub was called the Rose and Crown, and it was only a few minutes from the hotel, in a narrow passage off the thoroughfare of St Mary Street. It was exactly the kind of place Jack had described; both noisy and crowded. They sat in a corner that gave Jack a clear view of the rest of the bar, at his insistence, and for a while neither of them spoke. It was Michael who broke the silence, or whatever silence they had amidst the cacophony of the other patrons.

'So do you have any friends?' he asked.

Jack laughed. 'Friends? Well, there are people I know,' he replied. 'Associates, I suppose you'd call them. Acquaintances. I've had friends, but I've not seen any of them in a long time. You see, this thing I have, whatever it is I have… It doesn't lend itself to keeping friends.' He paused, and looked down at his pint of cold tap water with a wistful smile. 'It's like you're running on a different clock to everyone else. What feels like months to you is years to them, and then they're gone. They get older, they die. At first I'd go to the funerals, but then there were so many funerals to go to. The war didn't make that any easier.'

'You were in the war?'

'Oh yeah,' said Jack, nodding and still smiling. 'Both, actually, and a few more besides. And it's being in a situation like that that makes you… I don't know… think differently about it all. I mean, if life is so cheap that lives can be shovelled into war like… like lumps of coal into a furnace, what does that mean?' He shook his head, and took another sip of his water.

'You don't drink at all?' Michael asked.

Jack shook his head.

'Does nothing for me,' he said, grinning. 'I wish it did sometimes. You know, to take the edge off?'

Michael nodded. 'You do have friends,' he said. 'Not now, I mean, but in the future.'

'Whoa,' said Jack. 'No more. Like I said, you can't go telling me things that haven't happened yet. I could go into a whole lecture about paradoxes and upsetting the space-time continuum, and—'

'I know, you said,' Michael cut in. 'But just so you know. You *do* have friends. They seem like nice people.'

Jack looked back at his drink and smiled again. 'That's good,' he said.

Michael smiled at Jack and drank the last drops of beer from his glass. Unlike Jack he *had* been drinking, and the alcohol *was* beginning to affect him. He wasn't drunk, but his first two pints had definitely helped relax him, if only a little.

Even so, he'd not forgotten about his sister. He wasn't sure how he'd expected her to react but then, in hindsight, he'd never even known for sure that she would still be at the same address. He just wished things could have turned out differently.

To take his mind away from such thoughts, Michael looked around at the other men in the bar. It occurred to him that almost without exception there were no women in there, only men, and that the atmosphere was somehow different. It reminded him of one of the pubs back in Tiger Bay, a place he'd been to only once or twice. The men spoke differently to one another there, as if talking in some kind of code.

At the bar, he noticed an older man in a lilac shirt smoking a cigarette through a cigarette holder, talking to a surly-looking youth in a leather jacket. The older man giggled nervously at something the youth had said, and then placed one hand on his shoulder. There was something in the gesture that Michael recognised and understood. The older man was what Michael's father would have called a 'pansy' or a 'powder puff'. He knew that much.

'There's pubs like this,' said Michael, 'back where I'm from. In Tiger Bay. Some of the sailors go there.'

'What?' said Jack. 'You mean pubs where they sell beer?'

'No,' said Michael, bashfully. 'You know what I mean.'

Jack looked around the room, inspecting it, and frowned. 'No. I don't,' he replied.

Michael scowled. Was Jack mocking him?

'You *do*,' he said. 'Pubs for… you know… men who…'

Jack laughed. 'Oh… I *see*. Well, to be honest, I hadn't noticed. But it's true – I do have an uncanny habit of ending up in places like this. Nine star systems and many, many different eras, but it's always the same places, and often with the same faces. We can go somewhere else if you like.'

Michael shook his head. 'No,' he said. 'No, it's all right. We can stay here.'

Jack took another sip of his drink. 'So is there anyone else, apart from your sister? Are you married?'

'No,' said Michael, laughing nervously.

'A girlfriend?'

'No.' Michael paused, his mind momentarily elsewhere. 'Actually,' he said, 'there was a girl, Maggie Jenkins. We only went on one date. I don't know… It didn't go very well. Everyone in the pub kept saying I should take her out, but then when we went out it just didn't seem right.'

'OK,' said Jack. 'And was there anyone else before Maggie Jenkins?'

Michael scrunched up his nose and shrugged. 'There was someone,' he said. 'Someone I worked with, someone I liked, but I could never say anything to them. They were married, and… Well, I just couldn't.'

'And what's happened to them?'

Michael took a deep breath and looked straight at Jack. 'He died,' he said. 'In the accident. But like I said, I could never have told him. Chances are, even if I had he wouldn't have had a clue what I was talking about.' Michael shook his head. 'And now there's no one. And this thing keeps happening to me. I can't hold on to anything, it's all just slipping through my fingers like sand. What kind of a life is this?'

'It's just the life you've been given,' said Jack, softly. 'The only life.'

They walked back to the hotel a little after eleven o'clock that night. The darker streets of Cardiff were crowded with a night-time rush hour of vagrants and hookers, hustlers and spivs.

Michael could feel the effects of the beer now. He'd eaten and slept so little in what he supposed he should call the last few days that it hadn't taken much to leave him feeling drunk. As they entered the reception of the Shangri-La Hotel, the owner looked up at them and smiled.

'Evening, both. Capital city of Canada. Six letters. Something T something A something something.'

'Ottawa,' said Jack.

'Ah, that's it,' said the owner. 'I always thought it was Toronto. G'night lads.'

They climbed the four flights of stairs, the Shangri-La having been built in a time before elevators, and walked along the poorly lit corridor to the room. As they entered, Jack took a deep breath and clapped his hands together.

'OK,' he said, 'you can have the bed. I don't really need much sleep. I can just... you know... use the chair, or something.'

Michael looked at the rigid wooden chair and then at Jack.

'You don't need to do that,' he said.

FOURTEEN

When Michael woke, he was alone in the room. The whistling of trains leaving the station and the rumble of traffic in the streets outside had been his wake-up call and, looking at the clock on the wall, he saw it was only eight o'clock. But he was alone.

'Jack?' he called. There was no answer.

Michael felt his heart sink. So this was it. Jack had abandoned him in this hotel. He'd sensed something yesterday: a kind of desperation and fear that had been missing altogether from the Jack he'd met in another time. Jack had run away.

Breathing in, Michael could still smell him on the neighbouring pillow. It made him smile, if only briefly. Now, it would appear, he was alone again in another strange time and place.

He was standing beside the bed, slipping into his newly bought clothes, when the door opened, and Jack walked in, carrying a bag filled with groceries.

'Ah, you're awake,' he said.

'Jack…' said Michael, beaming. 'I thought…'

'You thought what? That I'd left you? That's crazy talk. I was just buying us breakfast. It's all fairly standard late-sixties British fair, I'm afraid. They're still a few years away from discovering the croissant, it would seem.'

'What's a croissant?'

'Exactly.'

Jack placed the bag down on the table and, as Michael stood, he pulled the young man close and kissed him. Michael flinched.

'Are you OK?' said Jack.

'Yeah,' said Michael. 'Of course. I just… It's just…'

Jack nodded.

'I see,' he said. 'It's the morning after, and you're feeling…'

'No, no it's not that. I just haven't… I mean… Before.'

'Really?'

Michael nodded, sitting on the edge of the bed to put on his shoes. He still looked puzzled, uneasy somehow.

'Never,' he said.

'I'm sorry,' said Jack.

Michael looked up at him and smiled.

'You don't have to be.' He paused to tie his shoelaces, and let out a short sigh. 'So… What are we going to do today?'

'Today,' said Jack, 'I'm going to ask some questions. And *this* time, I'm going to get some answers. But first, breakfast!'

As Michael ate, Jack stepped out of the room to use the

payphone in the corridor. Listening through the door, Michael could barely hear what he was saying, making out only the occasional sentence, and making sense of none of it.

'I can't. No… No. You don't have to worry about me doing a thing like that. It's nothing for you to concern yourselves with; it might be nothing. I don't know. A few days. A few weeks. What do you mean? The last time I checked, you don't own me.'

Jack hung up loudly, slamming the phone back into its cradle, and then came back into the room.

'Come on,' he said. 'We're going.'

'Who were you calling?' Michael asked.

'No one,' said Jack. 'Some friends. Acquaintances, really. Now come on…'

'Where are we going?'

'You'll see.'

Twenty minutes later, they were climbing the steps to the museum. Michael had seen it a hundred times or more, but still he paused and looked up in awe at the Doric columns and sculpted pediment.

'I've never been here before,' he said.

'You've never been to the museum?' Jack asked. '*Cardiff* museum? But you're from Cardiff.'

'I know,' said Michael. 'But my Dad always said it was for toffs and poofs. He said there was nothing in there for us.'

Jack shook his head.

'Sometimes you people amaze me,' he said. 'All this wealth of knowledge, all these beautiful things, all this history, and you just dismiss it as nothing. Come on. We're going in.'

'But why have we come here?' Michael asked. 'I mean, it's a nice building and everything but… Now? When all… all *this* is happening?'

'Ah, yes,' said Jack. 'Our lives are in flux. I can't think of a better time to see beautiful things.'

Walking across the vast entrance of the museum they neared a flight of steps in the centre of which was a dark statue of a young, naked boy, holding aloft what looked like a woman's head.

'What's that?' asked Michael.

'That,' said Jack, 'is Perseus. You ever heard of Medusa?'

Michael shook his head.

'She was one of the Gorgons, in Greek mythology. A monster with serpents for hair. She could turn people into stone just by looking at them.'

'Not all monsters are made up, though, are they?' said Michael.

Jack looked at Michael and shook his head. 'No. Not all of them.'

'And what about my monsters?' said Michael. 'What if they come for me again?'

'Well,' said Jack, grinning, 'this time they'll have to deal with *me*, won't they?'

Michael laughed.

'What's so funny?' said Jack, still smiling. 'I'll have you know I'm one tough cookie when it comes to duking it out with monsters…'

'It's not that,' said Michael. 'It's just that that's exactly what you said last time.'

Jack frowned, and then a moment later understood, and realised he already knew too much.

'Come on!' he said. 'Follow me!'

He climbed the steps in great strides, past the sculpture, towards the upper galleries of the museum, and Michael followed.

'But what's so urgent?' asked Michael, and then, with vague disdain, 'You said we were just looking at beautiful things.'

'True,' said Jack. 'But I also said we had questions that need answering. Who said we couldn't do both?'

They walked through gallery after gallery, past gaggles of schoolchildren listening attentively to prim and proper tour guides, and Michael looked at the paintings and wondered whether there would come a day when all of them would be gone for ever; burnt or buried like the pictures that had decorated his house when he was a child. Some of the paintings, so Jack told him, were centuries old; they had survived wars and plagues; but surely something as flimsy as canvas wouldn't last for eternity.

When he told Jack this, Jack felt a sudden stab of sadness. Michael had a point. Jack was beginning to realise that there was a very good chance he'd outlast every painting in the museum.

They'd walked through several of the larger galleries, when Jack said, 'There he is.'

'Who?' asked Michael.

'Sam,' said Jack, gesturing towards an old man with a mottled grey beard.

'And who's Sam?'

'He's the knower of all things,' said Jack. 'Like a kind of sage…'

'Like sage and onion?'

Jack laughed. 'No. Like a wise man. A magus. He's a friend, or as close to a friend as I've got most of the time.'

Michael looked at the old man and frowned. He didn't look all that special. In fact, he looked more like a tramp – sitting on one of the leather viewing couches with his shoulders slumped, his hands resting on a wooden walking stick, and an old and battered satchel at his feet.

On seeing Jack, the old man broke into a near-toothless grin. 'Jack!' he said.

Jack led Michael across the gallery to where Sam still sat. 'Sam, this is…'

'Michael,' said Sam. 'I won't get up, if you don't mind. Old bones. Can't get up and down too many times these days.'

His voice was deep, a soft growl like the voice Michael imagined an ageing lion might have if it could speak.

'It's been a while,' said Jack. 'How are you?'

'Oh, so, so,' said Sam. 'You know how it is. Never getting any younger. To what do I owe this pleasure?'

'I need a little information,' said Jack. 'About some names.'

Sam nodded and rested his chin on the top of his walking stick.

'I'll see what I can do, Jack,' he said. 'I'm not as sharp as I used to be. Things get cloudier the older you get.'

'I'm being followed,' said Jack. 'Any idea who it might be?'

The old man pursed his lips and glanced up at the ceiling, as if the answer might be floating somewhere in mid air.

'Yes,' he said. 'You're quite right, of course. But who? There's a warehouse. Near water. But it's not what it looks like, Jack. Inside... so many people. And so many rooms, and corridors. Oh, I'm sorry, Jack. Ten years ago, I'd have been able to walk you there myself, but now... What use am I?'

'It's OK,' said Jack, patting the old man's shoulder. 'It's fine. What about the name Hugo? Does that mean anything to you?'

Sam sucked air through his few remaining teeth and then smiled.

'Hugo Faulkner,' he said, nodding and drumming both hands on the walking stick. 'Posh lad? Talks like he's got a mouth full of plums?'

Jack laughed. 'That's him.'

'There's clouds there, Jack. Like storm clouds. But he's not the one you're afraid of...'

Jack shrugged this off and laughed through his nose. 'Afraid? I'm hardly a—'

'It's OK, Jack. You don't have to play the Humphrey Bogart act with me. How long have I known you?'

Michael looked at Jack and was surprised to see him blushing.

'OK,' said Jack. 'But can you see anything else? About Hugo?'

'Yes. He's not the one you're afraid of, but he doesn't know what he's doing. The man's as much of a fool as you think he is. There's a meeting? At the seaside?'

'Yes.'

'You want answers? Answers I can't give?'

Jack nodded.

'You'll go,' said Sam. 'To this meeting, I mean. And you'll get answers. They just might not be the answers to the questions you ask.'

Jack sighed. 'OK,' he said, 'I think I understand.'

'Oh, I doubt it,' said Sam, bursting into a hacking fit of laughter before covering his mouth with his fist. 'So,' he said, when he'd recovered, 'what about your young friend here?'

Jack put one arm around Michael's shoulder.

'He's like us,' said Jack. 'He doesn't really belong here.'

'Oh,' said Sam scowling, 'here? I belong here. Can't think where else I'd go. I'm ninety-six years old. Four more years and I'll get a telegram off the Queen. My pension just about pays for my tobacco and my bus fare in the mornings, and if I'm lucky I'll have enough left over for some liver and onions come teatime. Where else am I gonna go, Jack?'

Jack nodded.

Sam turned to Michael. 'You know,' he said, his watery blue eyes twinkling in the soft lights of the gallery, 'when I first met Jack, I was… how old was I, Jack?'

'You were thirty-one,' said Jack, smiling.

'Thirty-one,' said the old man, chuckling to himself. 'Thirty-one, indeed. I'd just come back from the Boer War, and I was just as lost as you are now, I'll wager. Now look at us. You'd reckon he was my grandson.' Sam looked down at his liver-spotted hands. 'It's a funny old thing, getting old. For those of us who do, that is.' And now he shot a smile at Jack and winked. 'Handsome devil, isn't he?' he said to Michael. 'Bit of a charmer too. Never went on in my day, of course…' And he winked again.

'OK,' said Jack. 'We need to go. But thanks. I'll see you around some time.'

Sam looked up towards the ceiling once more, his brow furrowed, and then back at Jack.

'Yes,' he said. 'You most certainly will.'

As they were about to leave him, Sam reached out and held Michael's hand.

'So lost,' he said, his face crumpling into a sad smile. 'But so brave. Safe travels, my friend.'

They were walking down the steps of the museum before Michael spoke again.

'What did he mean?' he asked. 'And how does he do that? How does he know things?'

'Because he's Sam,' said Jack. 'And sometimes it's best not to ask. Sometimes you just have to accept things as they are.'

Once they'd left the museum, they walked for a while around a nearby park, enjoying the last of summer, and Jack told Michael about the things that would happen in the world.

'Two years from now,' he said, 'man walks on the moon for the very first time.'

'The *moon*?' said Michael. 'Now I know you're making it up. The *moon*?'

Jack nodded. 'Uh-huh. He flies all the way to the moon. It takes them three days just to fly there, travelling faster than any car or plane ever did, on top of a giant rocket, and when he gets there, do you know what he finds?'

'Aliens?' asked Michael.

'No,' said Jack, laughing. 'He finds nothing. Just rocks, and a big black sky. You know, the moon is so small that when the first men are just standing there they can see its curvature, so that everywhere they look, it's curved, like they're just standing on this cold ball of rock in the middle of a black void. But do you know what else they can see?'

Michael shook his head.

'They can see the Earth,' said Jack. 'They can look up at the sky, and they can see the Earth, and they can blot it out with their thumb. Everything they know, every country, every single human being alive except themselves, and it can be blotted out with their thumb. But other than that, all they can see is black sky and that cold little rock.'

'So what's the point?' asked Michael. 'I mean, if there's nothing else up there. Why go?'

'Because they don't stop there. In a couple of hundred years there are ships, like the ships that you saw in the docks, only bigger, floating through the black sky, finding other places, and those places are much more interesting. Believe me… Boy, some of them are *very* interesting.'

'Hey…' said Michael. 'You told me I couldn't tell you anything about the future, and now you're telling me this.'

'I told you you couldn't tell me anything about *my* future,' said Jack. 'That's different. Nobody should know what's waiting for them. If you knew your future, why… it would take all the fun out of living.'

'But what about Sam? You asked *him* questions about the future.'

Jack frowned, looking up at the sky for an easy answer. Then he smiled and ruffled Michael's hair.

'Well, sometimes you have to cheat a little,' he said.

It was starting to get dark when they arrived on the inaccurately named 'Island' at Barry – in reality a peninsula that had long been linked to the mainland with the construction of the docks. A chilled late-summer breeze passed along the promenade, where Jack and Michael sat, looking out at the sea.

'Is it like this?' Michael asked. 'When you're looking out at space, I mean? Is it like when I'm looking at the sea?'

Jack nodded. 'Yeah, I guess,' he said. 'Depends what it's like when you're looking at the sea.'

Michael looked back at the ocean and frowned, deep in thought.

'It's like I can go anywhere,' he said after a while. 'Sometimes, when I was working, I'd be up on one of the cranes, looking at the sea, and it was like you could see for ever. I kept thinking maybe, if I squinted my eyes, I'd be able to see America, on the horizon, but I couldn't.'

Jack laughed. 'No,' he said. 'Well, America's a few thousand miles thataway.' He pointed out toward the horizon. 'And the Earth is round, so you won't see it.'

'Are you making fun of me?'

'No,' he said, laughing again. 'As if I would.'

'But that's what it was like,' said Michael. 'That's why I always wondered whether I should just join up with the Merchant Navy, get on a boat and go out there, go anywhere. I could see America, and China, and Japan. I could go places where I wouldn't feel so...' He shrugged. 'I don't know... different.'

'Yeah,' said Jack. 'I know that feeling.' He looked at his watch. 'Ten to nine,' he said. 'And it's already getting dark. Summer's almost over, I guess. Another summer, anyway.'

'How many summers have you seen, Jack?' asked Michael.

'A lot of summers,' said Jack. 'Too many to count. Some good, some bad. And on lots of different planets.'

'Really? You've *really* been to lots of different planets?'

Jack nodded, and Michael laughed.

'You know, a few days ago I'd have said you were gone in the head, but now... I don't know...' He looked up at a moon that was almost full, hanging on the darker edges of the sky. 'Two years?' he said. 'Two more years and man's walking on that thing?'

'Walking,' said Jack, 'playing golf, looking at the rocks. It's a start, at least.'

He looked at Michael with a soulful, almost apologetic gaze.

'I've got to go,' he said. 'To see people.'

'I'll come with you,' said Michael.

'Oh, no. You're staying here. I won't be long.'

'But you said you were going to ask questions and get answers,' said Michael. 'What if I've got questions? I'm tired of not knowing anything, Jack. I'm tired of running away from things, from people, and monsters. I'm tired of being on my own.'

Jack nodded.

'OK,' he said. 'But stay out of trouble. If anything happens, you run, OK? Don't worry about me.'

'I said I'm tired of running,' said Michael. 'And I meant it.'

They walked up an embankment towards the funfair. It had, Jack supposed, seen better days; rickety roller-coasters and a decrepit Ghost Train decorated with painted images of Boris Karloff and Bela Lugosi. The whole place was illuminated by the flashing lights of the rides and the amusement arcades, its soundtrack one of howling sirens, ringing bells, and the chaotic strains of 'Surfin' Bird' by The Trashmen. Any other night and Jack might have been able to cut loose and enjoy it for what it was worth, take in the sweet smell of hot dogs and candyfloss, and take it on its own terms, but not tonight. Tonight there was something sinister about the noise and the lights and the shuffling crowds.

'We came here once,' said Michael, 'when we were kids. Dad said we couldn't afford to come every year.'

But Jack was no longer listening; he was scanning the

faces of the crowd, looking for… looking for…

Hugo.

Hugo Faulkner stood beside the dodgem cars, still dressed immaculately in a pinstriped suit, holding an oversized lollipop. He'd been watching them the whole time.

Jack paced across the funfair and Michael followed.

'Jack!' said Hugo, smiling. 'And you've brought a little friend with you. How nice. Though that wasn't a part of our arrangement.'

'He's OK,' said Jack. 'He's with me.'

'Yes. I can see that,' said Hugo, and then, turning to Michael: 'Are you enjoying all the fun of the fair, young man?'

Michael didn't answer.

'Ah,' said Hugo. 'Silent and subservient. Just your type, eh, Jack?'

'OK,' said Jack. 'Now what?'

Hugo laughed, and took one lick of the lollipop, mashing his tongue against the roof of his mouth as if it tasted bitter. 'I never was one for sweets,' he said. 'Always more of a savoury person.'

'Cut this,' said Jack. 'I'm here, just like you said. What do you know about me? About who I am?'

'Hmm,' said Hugo. 'Not very gentlemanly or polite, Jack. I don't respond well to such blunt questioning. Follow me.'

They followed Hugo out of the funfair and back along the promenade, past holidaying families and elderly couples, until they came to the crumbling façade of the Empire Pavilion. A sign above its entrance announced a concert for a singer who had died some years ago, and the framed posters had all faded and curled in the sun. The doors were chipped and peeling, with broken windows boarded up by sheets of plywood.

'Beautiful building, don't you think?' said Hugo. 'A crying shame it's in such disrepair. Its days are numbered, I feel. Progress hates a ruin.' He reached inside his jacket and produced a small bunch of keys, checking each one in turn before holding one of them up. 'Ah,' he said, 'this one. Follow me.'

'We're not going in there,' said Jack. 'Anything could be in there.'

Hugo nodded sagely. 'Quite,' he said. 'Anything could, indeed, be in there. Answers, for example, could be in there.'

'What kind of answers?' asked Jack.

'Answers to your questions, Mr – oh, I'm sorry – *Captain* Harkness. So many questions which your little circle of friends seems unable or unwilling to answer. Answers regarding your inability to shuffle off this mortal coil, perhaps? Or might we find answers for your little time-travelling companion?'

Jack looked at Michael, and saw in his eyes the same look of anguished hope he knew he had in his.

'But of course,' said Hugo, 'if you choose to distrust me, you'll never find out. Will you?'

Jack sighed heavily, the only signal Hugo needed to

unlock and then open the peeling, graffiti-covered door. With his hand on his pistol, Jack followed Hugo into the cavernous gloom of the Empire Pavilion, with Michael close behind. For a moment they stood in impenetrable darkness, until Jack and Michael heard the loud clunk of a switch somewhere, and a number of lights flickered into life.

Compared with its worn and weathered exterior, the interior of the pavilion had a certain, threadbare glamour to it. With just the right amount of imagination it was possible to picture its halcyon days, when men in dinner jackets and women in evening wear might have passed through the doors for dinner and a dance, not so many years ago.

Hugo led them up a sweeping staircase and past a bar room full of upturned stools and tables before taking them down into the pavilion's ballroom. In the centre of the dance floor, beneath a single spotlight, three men and a woman sat around a small, round table. They weren't the kind of people Jack had been expecting. He'd expected a dozen more Hugos, with public-school voices and folded handkerchiefs in their breast pockets. These people were young, and dressed like students. The men had long hair and beards, and the woman was bedecked in beads and ribbons.

'This is our gathering,' said Hugo.

'These?' Jack said, laughing. '*These* are your friends?'

'They are,' said Hugo, flaring his nostrils. 'And what of it, Jack?'

'How old are you all?' asked Jack. 'Twenty? Twenty-one? I was expecting… Well, I don't know what I was expecting, but this? Beatniks? You've brought me here to meet a group of *beatniks*?'

'We're not beatniks, actually,' said a young man in a black polo-neck sweater with a peace sign pendant around his neck. 'We're revolutionaries.'

'Oh,' said Jack, 'you're *revolutionaries*. Well, excuse me, but this is one revolution that most definitely *won't* be televised.'

Hugo and the people around the table frowned.

'We know things,' said the man with the peace sign pendant. 'There are eye-witness testimonies. Albion Hospital, London, in 1941. Maidens Point in 1943. The Torchwood Estate in 1879.'

'Torchwood…' said Michael.

Jack turned to face him. 'You know that name?'

Michael nodded.

'We could continue,' said the woman in the beads. 'St Teilo's Hospital, 1918; Cardiff, 1869; the so-called "fairies" of Roundstone Woods… All evidence of paranormal activities and extraterrestrial visitors to this planet. All officially denied or debunked by Her Majesty's Government.'

'Well there's your answer, then,' said Jack. 'Denied and debunked. Did it ever occur to you that none of those things mean anything? That people might just be making stuff up?'

The people around the table laughed.

'Oh, come, come, Jack,' said Hugo. 'What use is there in denying it any further when you know that my friends here are telling the truth? There have been many unexplained goings-on this last century. Strange things that defy all logic, unless one applies an open and analytical mind to them. You, for example, Jack.'

'You're wearing very well for a man who must be, what, a hundred and twenty?' said the man with the pendant.

'OK,' said Jack, 'so just assuming you guys *are* onto something, what purpose does any of this serve?'

'We're here for the truth, Jack,' said Hugo. 'The British Government has made a number of important scientific – not to mention philosophical and political – discoveries this last hundred years. Discoveries it has kept a secret from the public, and from our neighbouring nations.'

'With good reason,' said Jack, coldly.

'Oh really?' said Hugo. 'And so it is down to the upper echelons to decide what is and isn't in the best interests of the country? Of the world? Come on, Jack, do you *really* believe that? I always thought you were a little more rebellious than that. You never seemed the Queen and Country sort. Well, certainly not the Country sort, anyway.'

'It's not about Queen and Country,' said Jack. 'Nobody benefits from knowing every secret there is. There would be mass panic. Confusion. Some things are best unknown.'

'Like weapons, Jack?' said Hugo.

'What's that supposed to mean?'

'These visitors haven't always come unarmed. They don't always "come in peace", as it were. And who gets to keep all those wonderful new gadgets and gizmos that they bring here? Are they disposed of, perhaps? Or are they stored, examined, and put towards the efforts of a belligerent few in the name of preserving their interests? Hardly seems like protecting lives then, does it, Jack? How many devices capable of killing hundreds, maybe thousands of people have been dismantled and redesigned by our clandestine organisations? How many new bombs that could put Hiroshima and Nagasaki in the shade have benefited from a little extraterrestrial help? One shudders to think.'

'So what are you going to do?' asked Jack. 'Talk to the newspapers? You know they won't listen.'

Hugo laughed. It was genuine and confident enough to make Jack feel uneasy.

'The press?' said Hugo. 'The venerable *fourth estate*? Oh please, Jack, don't make me laugh. The papers have little time for real news any more. They're too busy telling us about George Best and Brigitte Bardot to ever give us the cold, hard truth. No... There really is no point in us contacting the press with the information that we have. Better, I think, to level the playing field. When the Americans first developed the atom bomb, there were, thankfully, brave souls willing to transfer the information to their counterparts on the other side of the Iron Curtain. It is that information, Jack, which has prevented a holocaust that would make every massacre and genocide of the twentieth century so far look like a teddy bear's picnic. If both sides are so devastatingly armed, who dares fire the first shot? We intend to do likewise with any other-worldly information and technology that *our* authorities have.'

Now Jack laughed.

'And how are you going to do that?' he asked. 'What information do you have? What technology? You and your beatnik… I'm sorry… *revolutionary* friends are going to write to Kosygin and tell him you've heard some stories about flying saucers and little green men? That's great, Hugo. Really… That's hilarious.'

'We don't need to give them information or technology,' said Hugo, his smile fading to a cold sneer. 'We can give them you.'

Jack stopped laughing. From either side of the stage at the far end of the ballroom, men in heavy coats appeared, each carrying a gun. Jack turned to what he thought might be their only exit and saw more men entering the ballroom.

Leading the men was an incredibly tall woman with jet-black hair and intensely green lupine eyes, dressed in a long black leather coat and knee-high boots; a sense of innate style marred only by the Kalashnikov strapped to her side. She walked across the ballroom, smiling malevolently at Jack and, when she was merely inches away, and towering over him, Hugo introduced them.

'Tatiana, this is Captain Jack Harkness. Jack, this is Tatiana Rogozhin. She's with the Committee for Extraterrestrial Research, or the KVI, as it's known in Moscow. They are *very* interested in you, Jack. Very interested indeed.'

'You come with us,' said Tatiana.

Jack looked back at Michael, who was now surrounded by men with guns. He'd asked him to run, but it was too late now. He could run alone, of course. They could shoot him, and those bullets would have little or no effect, but that would still leave Michael. They were trapped.

'Now, Tatiana,' said Hugo. 'I know it might be rather vulgar of me to bring this up right now, but there is the matter of our payment. An organisation like ours doesn't run itself, as I'm sure you'll appreciate, and—'

Hugo didn't have the chance to finish the sentence. Tatiana turned on her heels, placing the barrel of the Kalashnikov under his chin, and fired a single shot up through his head in the blinking of an eye. Hugo's skull burst open with a sickening wet crunch, and his body slumped to the ground.

Around the table the self-proclaimed revolutionaries started screaming, getting to their feet and running for the exits. It was over in seconds, as each one was cut down in a streaming hail of gunfire from the foot soldiers. Tatiana turned to Jack once more.

'You come with us.'

FIFTEEN

The black Ford Transit sped through Tiger Bay in the pale blue light of the waning moon. Jack and Michael sat in the back, flanked on each side by Tatiana and her men, while in front and behind motorcycle outriders formed a convoy that snaked its way around the twisted narrow roads between the warehouses.

'You know something,' said Michael, smiling weakly, 'I'm starting to think monsters aren't that scary.'

Jack smiled back. 'You've got a point,' he said.

'Quiet,' said Tatiana. 'You'll talk later. When we tell you to.'

The van juddered to a halt, wheels crunching against gravel, and the back doors swung open.

'Out,' said Tatiana, tapping Jack's shoulder with her rifle.

Jack and Michael were pushed out into the waste ground between two large warehouses.

As they were marched towards the entrance to one of

the weathered grey structures, Michael looked up, above the gigantic doors, and gasped. Jack followed his gaze and saw the sign:

HAMILTON'S SUGAR

'What is it?' Jack asked.

'That name,' said Michael. 'I've heard it before.'

The doors to the warehouse opened with a metallic groan, spilling a sliver of yellow light out into their path, and Tatiana and the foot soldiers took them in.

Jack had seen the warehouse many times, but nothing had prepared him for what lay inside. It might once have been the warehouse for a sugar company, but it hadn't been used as such in a long time. There were crates and containers, sure, but all around the vast space were desks, telephones and, in one distant corner, an oversized Strela computer with whirring loops of tape and blinking lights.

'I guess the sugar trade must be having a bad year,' said Jack. 'Looks like they've had to branch out.'

'Quiet,' ordered Tatiana. 'This way.'

They crossed the hub of what Jack now realised was some kind of KVI substation, and were taken down a flight of steps into a subterranean network of corridors. Jack had heard of the KVI, of course. He made it his business to keep up to date on anything of interest, but even so the facts were hard to come by. He'd heard that the organisation was essentially a 1920s Soviet rebranding of a department set up under the Tsar some time after the Tunguska explosion in 1908, but very little more. What did the KVI want with *him*? Or with Michael for that matter?

They eventually came to two doors. One of Tatiana's men opened the first door and, clipping Jack in the small of his back with the butt of a rifle, pushed him inside before slamming the door shut. The second door was opened and, gripping him by the shoulders, Tatiana pushed Michael into the room.

'You wait here,' she said, grinning. 'We have a friend who'd like to see you.'

In the neighbouring room, Jack got to his feet and dusted himself off. He'd been in rooms like this before, but why did they always have to be so grubby? Why were they almost invariably underground? Why did they always smell of damp?

In the centre of the room there was a desk, to either side of which there was a single chair. An interrogation room, then, Jack surmised. Other than the furniture, and the bare bulb hanging from the centre of the ceiling, the room was featureless, devoid of any other purpose.

Jack crossed the room and placed one ear against the wall that connected to the next room. He hoped to hear something, anything, even if it was the sound of Michael crying. Michael had come to him for help, had come from nowhere, and now they were here, deep underground, and nobody except the KVI knew where they were.

He wasn't scared of death, of course, but that brought no comfort. There were, Jack had discovered, far worse things that death, and far worse things that could be done to Jack than killing him. It always plagued him that his enemies might use this to their advantage and, sometimes, when he found himself in idle thought, he'd think about how awful it might be to find himself with his feet encased in cement at the bottom of an ocean, or trapped inside a block of ice in the wastelands of the Arctic. He'd die, of course, over and over again, but his punishment would be like that of Prometheus, chained to a rock, forever being eviscerated by an eagle, only to wake up the next day and suffer all over again. He'd seen death up close, and he doubted there was much beyond it; any punishment for Jack had the potential to be infinite, unending. He'd never tell anyone this, of course, but Jack was scared.

Michael's room was similarly sparse and he spent his first few moments alone sat on the floor, where he had fallen, with his head in his hands. It was hard for him to feel despair; much of that had been used up these last few days. Now all that was left was pain and sadness. When he closed his eyes all he could see was the ballroom, its floor awash with blood and bullet-riddled corpses. He'd never seen death up close before, not even when his father had died. His memories of the explosion at the dock were cloudy; he'd seen little except that flare of light; but this time, in the ballroom, there had been blood. So much blood.

The door to his cell opened, and Tatiana entered with two of the guards.

'Get up,' she said, her husky voice echoing around the room. 'I said get up, and sit at the table.'

Michael stood and followed the order, unable to look at Tatiana. She was a terrifying combination of beauty and malevolence with an air of sardonic amusement; both seductive and deadly.

'We have a friend,' said Tatiana, 'who would like to speak to you.'

Michael looked out through the open door into the corridor, and saw a tall, angular figure emerge from the shadows.

It was Valentine.

'What to do with you, ay?' said one of the Russians, circling Jack like a vulture, his rifle constantly aimed for Jack's head.

'They say you can live for ever. Is this true, American? Is it true that you cannot die?'

Jack said nothing.

'I'd like to test that,' said the Russian. 'I could fire a bullet into your head right now and test that. Of course, Tatiana would never allow that. We need you.'

'Why?' asked Jack.

'They say you are special,' said the Russian. 'They say you are different. They say you have been many, many places and have lived a very long time. There are things you must know that would be very useful for our country. No?'

'I don't know what you're talking about.'

The Russian laughed. 'Oh, but we haven't even asked you what you know yet. Are you saying you know nothing? About *anything*? I doubt that very much. But who knows?

Maybe we are wasting our time here. Maybe everything they say about you is a lie, no? Maybe I should shoot you in that pretty little head of yours.'

'Are you flirting with me?' said Jack. 'Because, when I think about it, I don't think I've ever been with a Russian before. You might call that a glaring omission—'

The Russian struck him across the head with the butt of his rifle.

'Silence!' he yelled, grabbing Jack by the hair and slamming his face against the desk. Somewhere in the fog of pain, Jack wondered why his condition hadn't freed him of physical discomfort along with mortality. He put the back of his hand against his nose and taking it away saw blood.

The door of the cell opened, and Tatiana walked in.

'Ah,' she said, smiling. 'I see you are becoming better acquainted with Yevgeny.'

'I had no idea this was going to be a threesome,' said Jack, and Yevgeny slammed his head into the desk once more.

'Yevgeny is a good man,' said Tatiana. 'A good man, but… What is the word I'm looking for? Yevgeny, kak pa-Angleeski "izmenchiviy"?'

'Volatile,' said Yevgeny, leering at Jack.

'Volatile,' said Tatiana. 'He's a good man, but *volatile*.'

'Michael,' said Valentine, smiling warmly as he sat down at the desk. 'Fourteen years for us, but I'd say no time at all for you. You've changed out of those clothes but you're still a little boy lost in a big bad world.'

'Why are you here?' asked Michael. 'Where's the other one? Where's Cromwell?'

Valentine winced.

'Yes,' he said, 'I'm afraid we had our disagreements about the direction things should be going in. Then I had a better offer. Who would have thought it? Redistribution of wealth and all the rest of it, and yet our friends in Moscow are able to pay me more. But that's the problem when you switch sides, see? Your knowledge of the inside dries up, things move on. Times change, as I'm sure you know. Jack Harkness has seen and done things way beyond what many of us could imagine, and that's saying something. He's useful to us. His knowledge and experience are useful to us. But imagine my surprise when they said you'd tagged along for the ride.'

'But I don't know anything,' said Michael. 'I don't even know what's happening to me.'

'It's not what you know,' said Valentine. 'It's what you are.'

The butt of the rifle struck the side of his head once more, and this time Jack could feel blood, trickling down his cheek and along the contours of his chin. Yevgeny had tied him to the chair and was still circling him.

'Torchwood,' said Yevgeny. 'What do you know about Torchwood?'

'I've told you,' said Jack. 'I don't know anything about Torchwood. What's Torchwood?'

'On lozhnee,' said Tatiana: *He's lying*.

Yevgeny leaned close to Jack, so that his mouth was only inches from his ear and Jack could feel his breath.

'Tell us what you know about Torchwood. We want names. Locations.'

'How many times?' said Jack. 'I don't know what you're talking about. And if this is your way of trying to woo a guy, believe me, buddy, you're going about it the wrong way.'

Yevgeny laughed, and placed one hand around Jack's throat.

'You like that?' he said. 'You like it when I play rough, hm?'

His grip tightened, and Jack felt the swell of blood in his face. He looked Yevgeny in the eye.

'Oh yeah,' he croaked. 'That's it… Harder, baby, harder…'

Yevgeny glanced across at Tatiana, who was standing in a darkened corner of the room, watching with a cool impassivity. She nodded, and Yevgeny squeezed Jack's throat even tighter. Jack was feeling dizzy now, coloured spots dancing before his eyes.

'Is that enough for you?' said Yevgeny. 'I wouldn't want to crush your throat so bad you couldn't speak, now, would I? So is that enough?'

Jack shook his head as much as he could manage and forced a grin, though the pain was almost unbearable and he could feel himself slipping out of consciousness.

'I think you can go further,' he said. 'Go on… You know you want to…'

Yevgeny's eyes filled with rage, and he put both hands

around Jack's throat, crushing them together with every drop of strength he had until the tips of his thumbs drew blood.

As his world became entombed in darkness, Jack thought of Michael, of what they might be doing to him in the neighbouring room, and then he felt it again – that all-familiar surge and the cold embrace of the void.

He was still smiling at Yevgeny when he died.

'Massacres,' said Valentine, pointing at the array of black and white photographs and images of paintings and etchings from a bygone era that he had spread out on the desk. 'São Paulo in 1922. Canada in 1878. Japan in 1691. Siberia, 1927. Syria in the second century AD. Egypt in 1352 BC. All places where they were found… The spheres. Found, and then taken.'

'What are you talking about?' Michael asked. The photographs showed images of dead bodies, some barely recognisable as human.

'The crate that you helped us with in 1953 contained a metal sphere that was discovered in the Arctic about a hundred miles south of the Pole, buried beneath the ice, but it wasn't the only one. There have been others. The funny thing is, they never seem to last very long. They are discovered, transported, and that's when *they* arrive.'

'Who?'

Valentine smiled, the same lopsided smile Michael had first seen in the hospital, his mouth half-paralysed by the scar traversing the left side of his face.

'I think you know,' said Valentine. 'At least I should think you do by now. What do they look like to you, Michael? In Japan, they were said to resemble samurai. In Egypt they came "like gods". What do the creatures look like to you?'

Yevgeny checked Jack's wrist for a pulse one more time, waited, and then turned to Tatiana, shaking his head.

'Nothing.'

'Ha…' said Tatiana, staring into Jack's lifeless eyes. 'Maybe we were wrong. He's like the rest of us. Or rather, he *was* like the rest of us. Sweet dreams, *Captain* Jack Harkness. Take his body upstairs and have the men dispose of him properly. I want nothing left but ashes.'

'But what about the information?' said Yevgeny. 'If he's dead, he can't tell us anything.'

'There was no information,' said Tatiana. 'He was, how do they say, "taking us for a ride"? He was a conman, nothing more. Besides, if Comrade Valentine is to be believed, we've found something much better.'

Tatiana laughed, and walked out of the cell, the clacking of her heels echoing into the distance.

Yevgeny looked down at Jack's corpse and shook his head. Grumbling and swearing under his breath, he lifted the body onto his shoulder and carried him out of the interrogation room.

'So what are you going to do with me?' Michael asked.

'First,' said Valentine, 'Tatiana and her friends are going to put you on a boat. It arrives in a little under an hour.

Then they are going to take you to East Germany before transporting you to Moscow. It'll be a long journey, and not all that comfortable, but then again, you're no longer my concern.'

'And what's going to happen in Moscow?'

Valentine laughed coldly.

'They'll assemble a team of scientists,' he said, 'who will do their best to… *extract* whatever it is those creatures are looking for, whatever energy it is you soaked up in that explosion. Sounds like priceless stuff. *Powerful* stuff. The thing is, they need you alive. This has happened before, what's happened to you. Siberia. Exposure to one of the spheres left somebody in a very similar predicament. The patient died, and with it the energy just flickered out. Like *that*.' He clicked his fingers. 'So you don't need to worry about dying. Not yet, anyway.'

'Jack won't let you,' said Michael. 'He won't let you take me to Moscow.'

As he spoke, the door of the cell opened and Tatiana entered.

'Jack?' she said. 'You think your friend Harkness is going to save you? Oh, I'm very sorry to inform you that Jack Harkness is dead.'

SIXTEEN

Yevgeny had climbed three flights of stairs with a corpse on his shoulder and was now out of breath. He called two of the men, Pavlov and Mikhail, and ordered them to help him carry Jack to the furnace room at the back of the warehouse. They both nodded and, taking a leg each, dragged the body across the substation and down a dark and dismal corridor to the furnace room. There, they dropped it onto a metal workbench on the far side of the room, and all three began shovelling coal into the belly of the furnace.

'Make sure it's hot,' said Yevgeny. 'Tatiana said she wants nothing left.'

Inside the furnace, the flames roared into life, and Yevgeny began firing air into it with a small hand bellows.

'I hate this,' said Pavlov.

'Hate what?' asked Mikhail.

'Burning bodies,' replied Pavlov. 'The smell… It gets in your clothes, in your hair, in your nose. You can smell it for days. Weeks, even.'

'You should try working in the fish market,' said Mikhail. 'When I was a boy, I worked six days a week in the fish market in Berdjansk. You smell of fish all day, every day. Even Sundays.'

'Why can't we bury him?' Pavlov asked Yevgeny.

'Boss's orders,' he replied. 'She wants him burned. Only ashes left, she said.'

'Boss's orders…' said Mikhail, sarcastically. 'Always with the *boss's orders*. I'll be glad when I can leave this place and go home. There's no weather here. It never snows, it's never hot. Just rains all the time.'

'Hey!' cried a voice, in English.

The three men stopped what they were doing and turned to see the man who had been lying dead on the workbench now standing in the centre of the room.

Jack Harkness.

'Bozhye moy…' said Mikhail, crossing himself only a split second before Jack struck him across the head with a wrench.

Yevgeny dropped the bellows and reached inside his coat for his gun, but it was too late – the wrench hit him fully in the face, flinging him back against the side of the furnace. As Yevgeny fell to the floor, Pavlov too went for his gun and drew it, only to have it knocked from his hands with a single blow that broke several fingers. He fell to the ground, clutching his hand in agony. A final whack of the wrench left him sprawling unconscious beside his comrades.

'Terribly rude to start a party without me,' said Jack. 'Where are your manners?'

Valentine and Tatiana were now arguing in Russian, both shouting. It was Valentine who had started the argument, the moment Tatiana had entered the room and told them Jack was dead. Michael had stopped listening.

This was it, then. The only person who stood any chance of getting him out of here was gone. Everyone was gone. For a fleeting moment, he'd felt less alone and less scared. He'd felt safer, even in this terrible place, knowing Jack was nearby.

The boat was less than an hour from arrival, the boat that would take him to Germany before they moved him on to Moscow. He'd dreamed of leaving Cardiff, of course, of sailing to faraway countries, but not like this.

He was staring down at the ominous dark stains on the bare floor when he heard the door open with a loud bang, and then a single gunshot. When he looked up, Valentine was on the floor in a growing pool of his own blood, and standing in the doorway with a rifle was Jack.

'Harkness!' said Tatiana. 'You were dead… I saw you die…'

'Don't believe everything you see,' snarled Jack.

Tatiana raised her rifle and fired, but the hammer clicked on an empty chamber. She cursed, throwing the rifle to the floor, and began backing away from Jack, her tone changing very suddenly.

'Listen, Jack, it doesn't have to be this way. I'm sure we could come to an… arrangement?'

Jack swung his rifle, hitting her in the face, and she dropped to the ground.

He turned to Michael. 'What's the matter? You look as if you've seen a ghost.'

Michael leapt up from the table and ran across the room, flinging his arms around him.

'Whoa, there,' said Jack. 'Anyone would think you were pleased to see me.'

Michael looked at Jack, his heart racing, tears burning in his eyes. 'I thought you were dead,' he said. 'They told me you were dead.'

'Ah,' said Jack, 'what do they know?'

They kissed, and Michael held him as if he needed him to breathe. This time it was different. This time he didn't care about anything outside the room. All that mattered was that Jack was alive. He wouldn't have minded if that moment had lasted hours or even days, but it was cut short by the sound of an alarm.

'Do they know you've escaped?' asked Michael.

Jack shrugged, and then the two of them heard gunfire, from an upstairs room in the substation.

'That isn't for us,' said Jack. 'If it was, we'd be getting shot at right now.'

They ran from the cell and into the corridor to see two of the Russians standing at the far end, both of them with rifles.

'Ustanovka!' shouted one of the men: *Halt!*

As the Russians lifted their rifles to their shoulders and took aim, the fluorescent strip lights in the corridor began to flicker.

Behind them, an iron door first buckled with a loud

groan and then came crashing forward, blasted out by some unseen force.

'What is it?' asked Michael. 'What's happening?'

But Jack didn't answer. He was staring back down the corridor at whatever had been on the other side of that door. Michael followed his gaze and saw them, the men in bowler hats, exactly as they had appeared to him in so many other places, in so many other times. There were two of them, and they walked towards the two armed Russians, both grinning insanely. The Russians aimed at the creatures and fired, but it was as if the shots simply passed straight through them.

'Nam nada bezhat!' shouted the second Russian, and now both men ran towards Jack and Michael. Neither got very far. The Vondrax entered the corridor, and there was a noise like the hum of an amplifier, increasing in volume until one of the fluorescent strips shattered, and both Russians collapsed to the floor, their hands over their ears, howling in pain.

'What's happening to them?' asked Michael.

'I don't know,' said Jack, 'but we've got to get out of here.'

They were about to flee when the Russians' heads exploded in a cascading shower of gore, splattering both sides of the corridor. Their lifeless, decapitated corpses slumped to the ground.

'The Traveller...' hissed the Vondrax, in unison, stepping over the bodies.

'Go!' said Jack, taking Michael by the arm. 'Run!'

'Not without you,' said Michael. 'I can't go without you.'

Jack looked at him soulfully. 'You'll have to,' he said.

Michael turned and ran along the corridor until he came to another door, which led out onto a metal spiral staircase. He looked back at Jack just once before running up the stairs.

In the corridor, Jack faced the Vondrax. They were stalking closer and closer, the sound of their breathing like a death rattle. They looked human enough, from a distance, but up close they were quite clearly something else entirely. Everything about them looked diseased, from their sallow, desiccated skin to their hideous, carnivorous teeth. Why, Jack wondered, had they chosen to look this way?

As they drew closer still, their mouths fixed in rictus grins, black eyes behind black lenses, boring into him, he understood. It was fear. They liked to be feared.

'This one is different,' said one of the Vondrax, though there was no telling them apart. 'This one fears but does not die.'

'Kill it,' said the other Vondrax.

The first creature took off its round black sunglasses. It was now only two feet away from Jack, and he could see straight into its eyes, like polished ebony orbs in sunken sockets. A strange sensation gripped him, as if every nerve ending in his body were being shredded. It felt like dying, or rather, paradoxically, it felt like reliving every death he'd ever had.

'It feels pain,' said the first Vondrax, 'but it does not die.'

And then a strange thing happened. The first Vondrax made a noise in its throat as if it were choking. It stepped away from Jack, hunching over, its clawed hands bunched into white-knuckled fists. Black liquid began to pour from its open mouth and nose, hissing like acid as it hit the hard concrete floor.

The second Vondrax rushed forward, hurling its sunglasses to the ground, and picked Jack up by his throat. Again, like the first, it stared into his eyes.

'Cannot die?' it said, and then, as if it were analysing him: 'Curious composition. Why can it not die?'

An expression very suddenly appeared on its face that Jack hadn't expected. The Vondrax looked scared.

'The darkness…' it hissed. 'It sees the darkness…'

The Vondrax dropped him to the floor and it too began to choke, and then vomit out the same black ooze as the first. They were both now doubled over, their bodies shrinking away inside their suits, becoming ever more skeletal, their bones cracking and their skin flaking away as dust.

Jack ran from the corridor and up the metal staircase. Michael was waiting for him at a door two storeys up, holding it only slightly ajar.

'What is it?' Jack asked. 'What's happening?'

'They're everywhere,' said Michael, inviting him to look through the narrow gap between the door and the frame. 'They're *everywhere*.'

Peering through the gap, Jack saw the substation reduced to a scene of carnage. The foot soldiers were running, confused, in all directions, firing shots at the dozens of

Vondrax, who were impervious to their bullets. One by one, the guards fell; some spontaneously igniting, some ripped apart as if by invisible machinery. The stench of blood and burning flesh was overwhelming.

'We'll never get out that way,' said Jack. 'We need to get to the roof.'

They raced up the clanking metal stairs, higher up into the almost cathedral-like heights of the warehouse's upper levels. Below them the sounds of explosions and screaming continued, and the building shook with each blast, powdered concrete raining down around them in grey blizzards.

'It was like this once,' said Michael, 'in the future. I knew they'd come for me again, I knew it.'

Eventually they reached the top of the building, and a locked doorway that led out onto the roof.

'Stand back,' said Jack, and as Michael turned away and shielded his eyes Jack riddled the lock and the door with a dozen bullets. The lock exploded and the door was kicked open by the impact.

'Come on!' said Jack, running through the door and out onto the rooftop of the warehouse. Michael followed.

'What now?' Michael asked. 'Where can we go?'

'I hadn't actually thought that far ahead,' said Jack.

He ran to the edge of the building, looking down at the wasteland and the road between the warehouses. The Russians were swarming out of the building, yelling and screaming at one another. The Vondrax were following, picking them off one by one. Flames licked out of the shattered windows on lower floors, and somewhere in the depths of the building there was the menacing rumble of another explosion.

'Are we trapped?' asked Michael.

Jack ran to the other side of the roof and, looking down, saw a cliff-like sheer drop into the sea. They were too high up to jump and survive, and the water would be cold.

Michael followed him to the edge and looked down. 'We *are* trapped,' he said.

'Yes,' said a voice from the other side of the roof, and both Jack and Michael turned to see Tatiana, standing at the doorway, holding up her rifle. 'You are both quite trapped.'

'It's over Tatiana,' said Jack. 'Your men are dying. Those creatures are destroying everything.'

'But not you…' said Tatiana. 'They can't destroy you. I saw what you did to the others. You're different, Jack. And all I have to do is kill the boy and those creatures will go away…'

Jack stood in front of Michael.

'I won't let you do that,' he said. 'Tatiana… Face it. It's over.'

Tatiana lifted the rifle, gazing down its sights, and smiled but, before she could so much as pull the trigger, there was a terrible wet, ripping sound, and she was torn violently in half at the waist. As the two halves of her body were thrown in different directions, Jack saw three Vondrax, their lips curled back in sneers, needle teeth chattering frantically.

Michael turned away, and looking down over the edge

of the building he saw the moon reflected on the surface of the sea.

'They don't like mirrors,' he said. 'It's something Cromwell said… in the future. He said they don't like mirrors.'

'What do you mean?' said Jack.

'The water…' said Michael, pointing at the sea.

'No…' said Jack, shaking his head. 'If you jump from here you'll die.'

Michael nodded. 'I know.'

Jack shook his head again. 'No… no… You can't do that.'

'It's only over when I die,' said Michael. 'Cromwell told me that. And Valentine. If I die, this… this *thing* that they want… it goes. It'll be over.'

Across the rooftop the Vondrax were drawing closer with spider-like movements, their shapes transforming from suited humanoid figures into something bizarre and grotesque; reptilian scales appearing on their skin and writhing tendrils bursting from their torsos.

'I have to,' said Michael. 'I'm tired of this, now. I want this to be over.'

Jack pulled him close, holding him as tight as he could. In that moment, it was as if a part of him had always known Michael, as if their lives were in some way entwined for ever. He wanted the words of Cromwell and Valentine to be lies, just something they'd said, but he knew deep down that they weren't.

Michael pulled away from Jack and nodded. It was the

only way. He climbed up onto the wall, and looked down at the vertiginous drop, and then out toward the sea and the lights of distant ships.

'The Land of Horaizan,' he said, smiling softly.

'What's that?' asked Jack.

'It's something this little girl asked me,' said Michael. 'She asked me if I was from the Land of Horaizan. I thought she meant "horizon", but now I'm not so sure. Jack… What's dying like?'

Jack climbed up onto the wall beside him, and held Michael's hand.

'I wish I knew,' he said.

Together they fell nine storeys, a moment that to Michael seemed stretched out into infinity, a moment when he was always falling, when his whole life had been little more than a descent. They crashed through the surface of the water in an embrace and plunged deep down into the black sea, deeper and deeper until the light from the surface was barely strong enough for them to look into each other's eyes. Michael smiled, briefly, and then breathed out, his last breath rising to the surface in a volcanic storm of bubbles. Jack did likewise, and moments later they died in each other's arms.

The black Land-Rover ground to a halt before the burning ruins of the Hamilton's Sugar warehouse, the magnetic blue beacon light still flashing on its roof. As Cromwell stepped out of the vehicle, he saw that the place had already been swept by the army, something he was far from happy about, but then there was no plan in place for this. Tonight had taken them all by surprise.

It was embarrassing, truth be told, that a KVI substation could be in operation only a mile and a half from Torchwood and them not know about it. How long had this place been operational?

The few surviving Russians had already been cleared from the site, taken away in armoured cars by the ground crew, while a fire team now worked at putting out the flaming ruins. Cromwell guessed that the whole site would be one big waste ground within a few hours, all evidence of the events that had taken place that night taken away for analysis or bulldozed into the sea. The incident at Hamilton's Sugar would never have happened. At least not officially.

Pausing to light a cigarette as he surveyed the destruction, Cromwell turned to the woman who had driven the Land-Rover; a tall brunette in a black miniskirt and leather jacket. She was already taking readings, walking around the rubble and the patches of blood where bodies had been, pretending not to notice the lustful looks from some of the soldiers.

'Lucy?' said Cromwell. 'Anything?'

'Nothing,' Lucy replied. 'They're gone.'

'All of them?'

She nodded.

Cromwell took a long drag on his cigarette and shook his head.

'So much death,' he said.

He was walking towards the edge of the quayside when two soldiers approached him, carrying a covered body on a stretcher.

'Sir, Captain Turner said you might want to see this,' said the first, indicating the body.

Cromwell nodded, took another drag on his cigarette, and lifted the sheet. Though covered in blood and ash, one side of the face partly staved in by falling masonry, it was the scar that identified the corpse. Valentine was dead.

'So it goes,' said Cromwell. 'Goodbye, Mr Valentine. Take him away, boys. Do with him what you will.'

Cromwell sat, a little awkwardly, on one of the mooring posts on the edge of the dock. Age, he felt, was starting to creep up on him. There had been a time, which didn't feel so long ago, when he would have been the one running around the ruins, noting every last detail, taking readings. He'd have shrugged off, or at least blocked out, the more gruesome details, like the pools of blood or the recognisable fragments of tissue and bone. Those days were leaving him now. How much more of this did he have left in him? Five years? Ten?

His moment's contemplation was interrupted by the sound of splashing water. He turned around suddenly, and looking down at the sea saw a figure emerging from the surface. It was a man, a man who gripped a rusting ladder with both hands and pulled himself, gasping as if in pain, up onto the edge of the dock. For a moment he lay there, on his side, coughing up water and simply staring into space, as if his mind were a million miles away.

'Harkness…' said Cromwell, but the man did not acknowledge him. Instead, he got to his feet and walked away, past the ruins of the warehouse, past Lucy, leaving a trail of wet footprints behind him.

'Jack?' called Cromwell, but it was too late.

Jack Harkness was gone.

SEVENTEEN

Jack's office was silent but for the whirr of his computer. He hadn't spoken in perhaps a minute. Ianto leaned back against one of Jack's archaic filing cabinets, drumming his fingers on one of the metal drawer fronts, and sighed.

'But Valentine?' he said. 'Why did they wipe all his records?'

'Embarrassment?' said Jack. 'Desperation? I don't know. They were different times. There weren't just aliens and the Rift to think of.'

Jack was quiet now. He wasn't in the mood for questions. As he'd told Ianto about the events at the KVI substation, he'd glanced occasionally at his monitor, and at the image of Michael, sleeping. The whole night had felt like a cruel dream; the kind of dream you have in which a loved one who has died comes back and, halfway through, you recognise it for what it is: a lie.

'But it's worse than a lie,' thought Jack, 'because it's a lie you tell yourself.'

'So where does this leave us?' asked Ianto.

Jack looked at him quizzically. 'What's that supposed to mean?'

'I mean, if he's here now…'

Jack shook his head. 'He won't stay,' he said. 'The guy sleeping down in the Boardroom… None of those things have happened to him yet. He's still alive, for one thing.'

'But maybe you could stop it… I mean…'

'No,' said Jack. 'Not in this universe. In this universe, Michael always goes back to 1967. He always dies.'

'So there's nothing we can—'

'No.'

Ianto thought about this for a moment. He'd been thinking of Lisa, ever since he'd told the others about his encounter with Cromwell at Torchwood One. Those days seemed a lifetime ago, now. Lisa seemed so many lifetimes ago.

'You need to go to him, then,' he said. 'Now, I mean. Go and talk to him. Just… just *be* with him.'

Jack nodded, and smiled. As he walked out of his office, Ianto caught his hand, and held it for a second before letting go.

'So these Vondrax?' said Gwen. 'They look like people?'

Toshiko shrugged. She was examining the Orb, while Gwen sat at her workstation sipping coffee that was still a little too hot.

'Kind of,' she said. 'I can't remember. Or at least I couldn't remember. Until now.'

'And they wear bowler hats?'

Toshiko nodded.

'But why?' said Gwen. 'Why do you think they wear bowler hats?'

'I don't know. To fit in?'

'It's weird. It just reminds me of something Jack said a while ago. He said that in an infinite universe there must be a planet full of civil servants. Maybe that's the planet they're from...'

Toshiko laughed softly. 'I've seen one of them, Gwen,' she said, 'and they were *not* civil servants.'

Then she looked at Gwen with an expression serious enough to kill Gwen's smile. She looked strangely scared, as if the memory were enough to still terrify her.

Jack stepped out of his office and walked across the Hub.

'Having fun?' he asked. It was the kind of line that would normally be accompanied by a smile, but he said it softly with little trace of emotion.

Toshiko looked up from the Orb. 'This thing,' she said. 'There's no tech. No moving parts. The metal is a new one on me.'

'Have you named it yet?' asked Jack.

Toshiko frowned. 'What do you mean?'

'Well, it's a new metal. Nothing like it on Earth. You should name it. Something like Toshikinum. Or Torchwoodium, if you're not into the whole egocentric naming thing.'

'Torchwoodium it is,' said Toshiko. 'I just can't figure out how it works. Or rather, how it *worked*.'

'And I don't think you ever will,' said Jack. 'That thing is probably older than this planet. Maybe older than this solar system. The creatures that made it were working with technology as old as the stars themselves. It's Clarke's Third Law, Tosh. Clarke's Third Law.'

'You said that earlier, Jack. What's Clark's Third Law?'

'I'll tell you some other time,' said Jack. 'I have to go see how our visitor's doing.'

As Jack headed down towards the Boardroom, Toshiko left the Orb on the table and followed him.

'Um, Jack,' she said. 'I've been thinking…'

Jack turned. 'About what?'

'Well, about the Vondrax. If they follow Michael, and Michael's here…Well… What do we do if they turn up?'

Jack breathed deeply. He could still see the Vondrax in the underground corridor of the KVI substation, and the bullets passing through them as if they were made of smoke. He'd been immune to them, but the others hadn't been so lucky.

'They don't like mirrors,' he said, glancing across the Hub, and Toshiko followed his gaze.

'I wonder,' said Owen, peering through the glass of the holding cell. 'Do you have regrets? Do you sit in there sometimes and think, "How the bloody hell did I end up here? What did I do to deserve living in this little bloody room a hundred feet below Cardiff?"'

In its cell, Janet was hunched over in one corner, breathing quietly but for the occasional grunt. It was hard to know whether the Weevil was listening to him or not and, if it was, whether it might be able to understand a single word he was saying.

'I wonder what you think of us,' said Owen. 'I mean, apart from as food, obviously. I wonder whether you've got a favourite.'

Janet looked at him, its deep sunken eyes peering out of the shadows, recessive glints of light almost lost behind its gnarled, bestial features.

'I bet I'm your favourite,' said Owen. 'The amount of time I spend down here. Our little chats. Well, I do all the chatting, you just seem to sit there and grunt, but that's OK.'

Owen tapped his feet on the floor and laughed softly. Sometimes, when he was down in the Vaults, he'd see himself, as if having an out-of-body experience, and find the whole scenario ridiculous. It was, of course, ridiculous, and yet there was still something strangely comforting about it. Some people paid for therapy. Owen had Janet.

Michael was waking as Jack entered the Boardroom. He sat up on the inflatable mattress, yawned and rubbed his eyes.

'I'm still here,' he said, smiling.

'Yep,' said Jack. 'You're still here.'

Michael looked around the room and then at Jack.

'I wonder how much longer,' he said. 'First time I was only there five minutes. Then the next time it was hours. How long have I been here?'

Jack looked at his watch. 'Just over three hours,' he said.

'It's getting late.'

Michael frowned. 'Is it?' he said. 'I didn't know what time it was. You don't have any windows.'

'No,' said Jack, laughing softly. 'We wouldn't.'

There was a long silence between them, a silence that was strangely comfortable, Michael thought, for two strangers.

'So,' said Jack. 'Are you hungry? Thirsty? Is there anything I can get you?'

'No,' said Michael. 'I'm OK. I'm still a little queasy. It's the… the *thing*. When it happens. It always leaves me feeling a bit sick.'

Jack nodded. 'Anything you wanted to do?' he said. 'Maybe watch a little twenty-first-century TV? I mean… It's not that great. Mostly repeats and celebrities dancing. And talent shows.'

'No,' said Michael. 'It's OK.' He paused and then looked up, his face illuminated by an idea. 'Actually, I was thinking. Maybe you could take me outside?'

'I don't know…' he said. 'Maybe it would be better if—'

'Oh please,' pleaded Michael. 'You said we were in Cardiff. I'd like to see what it's like. Now, I mean.'

'OK,' said Jack. 'You win. But no running off anywhere. And you'd better prepare yourself for a bit of a shock.'

Ten minutes later, Jack and Michael were standing on the platform at the base of the water tower.

'Is this thing safe?' asked Michael.

'Oh yeah,' said Jack, laconically. 'We'd never be allowed to have one of these things if it didn't stand up to all the…

you know… rigorous… er…'

The platform began to rise up above the Hub.

'Rigorous what?' asked Michael.

'Oh, you know,' said Jack. 'Health and safety stuff.'

Michael stood a little closer to Jack and a little further from the edge of the platform as they passed up through the ceiling of the Hub and, seconds later, found themselves standing in front of the Millennium Centre.

'Where are we?' Michael asked.

'Michael Bellini…' said Jack. 'Welcome to Cardiff.'

Michael looked up at the colossal steel dome of the concert hall. Walking around the base of the water tower, he saw the stream of streetlights leading off to a vanishing point on Lloyd George Avenue, and then the piazza of restaurants on the other side of the square. When he'd come full circle, he saw the lights of the barrage reflected on the sea, and then the floodlit façade of the Pierhead Building.

'I'm home,' he said, laughing to himself. 'It's Tiger Bay, isn't it?'

Jack nodded.

'That's right,' he said. 'You're home. Let me show you around.'

Ianto didn't look himself. Gwen had never seen him look this way before. His stoicism, his trademark Ianto Jones imperviousness, had faded somehow.

She rapped her knuckles on the door of Jack's office, and Ianto looked up.

'Penny for your thoughts,' asked Gwen.

'Cheapskate,' said Ianto. 'Never heard of inflation? Thoughts are a bit pricier than that these days.'

'OK,' said Gwen. 'A pint down the local tomorrow for your thoughts?'

Ianto smiled. 'That's more like it.'

'So...?' said Gwen. 'What's on your mind?'

'It's nothing,' said Ianto. 'Just tonight.'

Gwen understood. For a quiet Sunday night, and compared to some Sundays it *had* been quiet, the last few hours had been an emotional experience, though not necessarily an unhappy one for her. She'd forgotten all about the argument in the sofa shop, and was now thinking of home, and Rhys.

'Did Jack tell you anything?' Gwen asked. 'I mean about Michael?'

Ianto nodded. 'Just when you think you know him...'

'I know. Tell me about it.'

Gwen smiled, but she couldn't help but feel a pang of jealousy that Jack had opened up to Ianto and not her. Hadn't there been a time, not so long ago, when they would have shared such things? Weren't they still close?

Jack's time away had put a strain on the whole team, it had changed things, there was no doubting that, and tonight had brought a peculiar focus to this. Jack was like a box full of secrets sometimes, and every time a new box was opened it seemed to contain another box, like ever-diminishing Russian dolls.

Owen hadn't spoken for a while. It was unlikely the others would bother him while he was down here, which gave him time to think clearly, without distraction. He thought about the friends he had made at the hospital; people he very rarely saw these days. He'd been convinced, in his youth, that he'd know those people, the other trainee doctors, his colleagues, for the rest of his life. He'd see them every now and then, of course – it was hard not to in a city the size of Cardiff – but they had little to talk about. He'd tell them he was working on a research project, but keep it intentionally vague.

If he told them what he did, day-in day-out, he imagined they'd probably think him insane, but even if they *did* believe him, he thought they'd probably pity him. They'd never quite be able to understand the part of him that *loved* this, that thrived on it. They'd never understand his reasons or his rationale, and they certainly wouldn't understand why *he* pitied *them*.

He was about to leave the holding cells when the lights flickered once, then twice in quick succession, and Janet, staring up at the ceiling, let out a long, mournful howl. He'd seen the Weevil act this way before, of course, but this time it was different. Something was very wrong.

Toshiko crossed the Hub with a cold can of Coke, pressing the can gently against her eyes. It was something she did when she was tired and her eyes were beginning to feel puffy. She doubted whether it had any particular scientific benefit, but it always seemed to wake her up.

She'd looked up Clarke's Third Law on the internet, after Jack had gone to the Boardroom, hoping it would give her some kind of answer to the mystery of the Orb, but it didn't. Clarke's Third Law was the kind of thing only a sci-fi nut would know. A sci-fi nut, or Jack Harkness.

Any sufficiently advanced technology is indistinguishable from magic.

She laughed when she read that, and went back, still laughing, to the Orb. How could something so small, so seemingly insignificant, contain so much power? Even with her scientific, investigative mind, it still puzzled her. How had all that energy got in there? How and why did it get out?

It was too late for her to be asking these questions. She knew that. No matter how many times she dabbed her eyes with the ice-cold surface of the can, she needed to sleep. Sleep was often a luxury at Torchwood. She'd lost count of how many times a night of slumber had been interrupted with a phone call and word of some imminent catastrophe in another part of town. Toshiko had begun to think of holidays as quaint things other people had.

She was about to shut down her computer and pack up for the night when she felt an icy chill on the back of her neck and heard an all too familiar voice say her name.

'Toshiko…' the voice rasped. 'I smell something sweet.'

'I just can't believe it,' said Michael, running down towards the water's edge. 'That – over there – that would have been the place where all the bananas used to come in. They used to come in from Brazil in those days. And over there…' He laughed. 'Over there was this place, you know, where the sailors would go when they were on shore leave for a bit of how's your father…'

Jack could hardly keep up with him, but for a moment it was as if all his memories of that night, over forty years ago, had faded, like a bad dream. Michael looked almost happy.

'But where are the docks now?' Michael asked. 'I mean, if this is all fancy bars and restaurants, and that bloody great big opera house, where's the docks?'

'They're gone,' said Jack. 'They went a long time ago.'

Michael's ebullience waned and he stopped running.

'Really?' he said. 'Everything's gone?'

'Things change. The world changes. People change.'

Michael nodded pensively, and then walked slowly along the waterfront, gazing out over the sea.

'That's where I worked,' he said, pointing out across the water at a distant headland. 'That's where we all worked.'

He leaned against the black railings and smiled wistfully at the lights on the water. He'd thought, for a moment, that he was home, but he knew deep down that home was very far away.

Owen raced up the steps and into the Hub only for something to hit him full force in the chest, flinging him back against the wall. As he gathered his senses and looked up, he saw them for the first time.

The Vondrax.

One of them held Toshiko in the air by her throat, while two more were methodically stalking around the Hub, tilting their heads in a curious, almost childlike fashion, as they examined each workstation. One of them came to the Orb, and picked it up as if it weighed next to nothing.

Owen's gun was in its holster, but that holster was slung over a railing in the Autopsy Room. He cursed himself for leaving it there but, as he tried to stand, that same invisible force struck him once again, pinning him down. One of the investigating Vondrax turned to him, lips curled back, its rows of metallic, pointed teeth gnashing together, and it smiled. The thing actually *smiled* at him.

'Stop!'

He heard Ianto's voice and, from his corner of the Hub, Owen saw Ianto and Gwen, both with their guns aimed squarely at the Vondrax.

'Put her down,' said Ianto, Jack's words racing through his mind – his description of how bullets had passed straight through the Vondrax. Any effort now, Ianto felt, would be pointless. What could they do?

'The Traveller…' said the Vondrax, still holding Toshiko by the throat. 'Where is he?'

'Put her down!' Ianto shouted again. He was stalling, he knew that he was stalling, but what else was there? Where was Jack?

One of the Vondrax was now peering into Toshiko's monitor, tilting its head first left, and then right. On the screen there was a CCTV image of two men walking across the piazza outside: Jack and Michael. The Vondrax tapped the screen twice with its clawed index finger.

'The Traveller,' said the Vondrax that held Toshiko before hurling her to the ground and vanishing in a sudden blur. Toshiko got to her feet and ran across the Hub to the others. The remaining Vondrax followed her.

'I wonder how long I've got left,' said Michael. 'Here, I mean. Now. How does all this end?'

Jack couldn't answer him. He'd told him, so many years ago, that it was wrong to know your future. That rule didn't just apply to finding out lottery numbers or sports results. Even so, knowing the importance of that didn't make it any easier.

'I don't know,' he said softly. 'Maybe somebody will find a way home for you.'

He turned to Michael. He wanted to say and do so much more.

'I just wish it could have been me.'

'Jack!' Michael shouted. He was looking over Jack's shoulder, at something in the distance, his face suddenly a frozen mask of fear. Jack span around and saw, on the edge of the piazza, a man in a black suit and bowler hat, walking towards them. He turned again and saw three more on the other side of the square.

'It's them,' said Michael. 'They're here again. They've come for me, haven't they?'

'It's OK,' said Jack, standing between Michael and the Vondrax. 'This time they'll have to deal with me.'

They edged their way back across the square. Looking in every direction for an escape route, Jack saw another Vondrax appearing, until finally he could no longer count them. They were marching forward, forming an ever-tightening circle around the two men.

They never ran. That was, perhaps, what disturbed Jack most about them. It was as if they never *needed* to run. As if they knew they would always get you in the end.

One of the Vondrax had advanced on them and was now only feet away. It looked at Jack with a strange kind of curiosity, as if sizing him up, before very slowly removing its sunglasses. Jack and Michael were still edging their way back toward the water tower, and Jack had drawn his pistol, though he knew it was pointless.

'Give us the Traveller…' said the Vondrax, smiling and hissing.

Jack laughed, causing the Vondrax to grimace and then frown, as if it had been able to taste his derision. It stepped closer again, now staring into him with its melanoid eyes, and Jack felt a familiar surge of pain from one end of his body to the other, every nerve once more being twisted, but he wouldn't give in.

The Vondrax made a self-satisfied gurgling noise in its throat, a sound cut short as its expression changed quickly to one of horror.

Black fluid, like liquefied tar, began to pour from its eyes, and then its nose, and its skin began to crack and tear, with more dark sludge spilling out from the cracks.

'The darkness!' it hissed. 'The darkness!'

As its whole body buckled and twisted on the ground, Jack turned to Michael.

'Close your eyes,' he said. 'Don't look at them… and follow me!'

Jack grabbed Michael by the arm and together they ran across the square, the circle of Vondrax growing tighter still. He dragged him to the water tower, with its reflective metal surface, and they stood with their backs against it.

Seeing their reflections in the surface of the tower, the Vondrax hissed, covering their eyes, but they didn't come any closer.

'Ha!' said Jack. 'How d'you like that, huh? And they say public art serves no purpose. I knew it would come in handy one day.'

'What's happening?' said Michael. 'Why are they just stopping?'

'Because,' said Jack, almost out of breath, but smiling, 'they don't like mirrors. Something to do with the waveform they use to kill, but it's more than that. They've been around so long they can't stand to look at themselves in the mirror. Well, that's my theory, anyway.'

'So what do we do now?' said Michael.

Jack's smile faded. 'That's a good question. That's a very good question.'

'And…?'

Jack laughed. 'I'm sorry, Michael. I'm a little out of ideas right now. But at least that's about as far as they're gonna get.'

He hated this. He hated the helplessness. He'd wanted

to protect Michael, just this one time, but here they were again, stuck in a hopeless and helpless situation. How much longer could they stand there, with their backs against the water tower? They couldn't go down into the Hub; the Vondrax would follow.

'It's OK, Jack,' said Michael. 'I think it's going to be OK.'

Jack turned to him. What did he mean?

'I think it's happening again,' said Michael, smiling. 'I can feel it. I'm going again.'

'No,' said Jack. 'No. Stay. This time stay.'

Michael shook his head. 'I can't. I can't control this.'

'Try,' said Jack. 'Just this time, *try*. Please.'

Michael laughed bashfully.

'You're funny,' he said, shaking his head. 'Anyone would think you were going to miss me.'

'No,' said Jack. 'Don't g—'

But it was too late. Jack blinked and, in the split second that his eyes were closed, Michael vanished. A second later, the air around the Vondrax appeared to fold, as if they were slipping back through gashes in space itself, and Jack was alone with just one thought.

What about the others?

'OK,' said Owen. 'So we've worked out they don't like mirrors. Now what?'

The four of them were gathered at the base of the water tower, facing out into the Hub, and surrounded by Vondrax. The creatures clawed at the air, hissing and snarling but unable to advance.

'I don't know,' said Toshiko. 'That's all Jack said. They don't like mirrors.'

'So we could be stuck here for how long, exactly?' said Owen. 'Hours? Days? You see, I could *really* do with a pee about now…'

'Owen,' said Gwen. 'You're not helping.'

'So you got any ideas?' said Owen.

Gwen scowled at him and then looked back at the Vondrax. They were studying the water tower now, and glancing around the Hub, as if trying to work out some way of destroying the thing that was holding them back. How much longer did they have left?

'Hey!' A voice from the other side of the Hub. A familiar voice.

One of the Vondrax turned around, and came face to face with Jack Harkness.

'This is private property,' said Jack. 'I'm going to have to ask you gentlemen to leave.'

He reached out and grasped the Vondrax by its throat, his fingers sinking into its flesh, its oily blood spilling out over his hands. The creature writhed in agony, a high-pitched scream emanating from its gaping mouth, its limbs cracking with each contortion. The other Vondrax turned away from the water tower and launched an attack, but they too were seized with agonising convulsions, their bodies breaking up before Jack's eyes. As the screaming of the Vondrax reached an almost deafening pitch, the Hub was shaken by a series of crashing sounds, like thunder, and bolts of flashing energy exploded from the decaying bodies of the Vondrax, vaporising each and every one of them.

Jack stood in the centre of the Hub, looked down at his hands, and sighed. It was over.

'Jack,' said Gwen. 'What was that? What happened?'

Jack crossed the Hub in silence.

'So where is he?' asked Owen. 'Michael, I mean?'

Owen was angry; a walking embodiment of rage, but Jack had little time for it.

'He's gone,' said Jack.

'Gone? Gone where?'

'He's *gone*.'

'And what if those things come back? Because it struck me that there was bugger all we could do except stand with our backs against that thing.' He pointed at the water tower.

'You're right,' said Jack. 'That's all you *could* do. They don't like mirrors. I'm glad Tosh took the hint.'

'So no plan B, no get-out clause… We were stuck with our heads up our arses not knowing what to do.'

'You were lucky,' said Jack.

'Lucky?' asked Owen. 'You try telling that to Tosh. She's not feeling very lucky.'

Jack stopped in his tracks and turned to Owen, staring him down.

'You were lucky,' he said again. 'They don't usually leave survivors.'

'Well that's reassuring,' said Owen, sarcastically. 'And what if they *do* come back?'

'They're not coming back,' said Jack. 'They were here for Michael, and Michael's gone.'

'Oh yeah?' said Owen. 'And didn't you think you'd seen the back of him *last* time? How many more secret friends of yours are we going to meet, Jack? How many more skeletons have you got in your cupboard?'

Jack, now standing in his office, turned to face Owen one last time, and slammed the door shut.

EIGHTEEN

Ianto Jones sat down with a hot cup of coffee and kicked off his shoes. It was nearly one o'clock, but he wasn't tired. Adrenalin did that to him. It was better than caffeine, though he'd rather drink coffee than go through another experience like tonight's.

Jack had left the Hub without saying a word to him, and soon the others too had called it a night. Now he was alone, but Ianto didn't mind so much. He'd always thought there was something reassuring, something protective about the Hub, as if it were his own subterranean cocoon, and, though it made him chuckle to think so, he liked having the place to himself. It wasn't a flashy Docklands apartment, but for now at least it was pretty close to being home.

He hit 'play' on the remote control, and seconds later, and without a trace of self-consciousness, said, 'No, Mr Bond, I expect you to die', in perfect synchronisation with the film.

Owen Harper walked home that night. The city's streets were now almost deserted in the aftermath of a Sunday night; fast-food cartons clogging the gutters, broken bottles and spilt takeaways next to the taxi stands. A few clubs were still open, bass-heavy music blasting from their open doors, gaggles of smokers standing on the pavements puffing away like little steam trains, revellers with presumably no early start the next day.

It crossed Owen's mind that once upon a time he would have gone out. Maybe had a few drinks, to take the edge off and help him sleep. Maybe he'd have met someone. Anyone. Maybe he'd have met a girl, taken her home, and then put her in a taxi in the morning.

He stopped outside the entrance to one club, eyed the surly bouncers and the small queue of drunken teenagers, looked in through the doors at the flashing strobe lights, and then carried on walking.

The underside of Toshiko Sato's bed was a miniature cityscape of shoeboxes, each one covered in a fine layer of dust. It always shamed her a little to look at this untidy, cluttered corner of her life but, so long as it was hidden from plain view, she didn't mind so much.

She reached under the bed, sprawled across the mattress, leaning upside down over its edge, and dragged out one of the boxes. Lifting off the lid she took out one of the photograph albums that were stored inside and, sitting back on the bed, began to flip through its pages.

The photos inside had that certain, almost sepia quality

that old photographs have – all faded and desaturated hues. There were photographs of her parents' wedding day, and of her mother cradling her in the hours after she had been born. There were images of their home in England, and of her first birthday party, with Toshiko sat in a highchair, staring bewildered at the single candle on a cake in the shape of the number 1. Then there were the pictures of their apartment in Osaka, and her grandmother, always sat in her favourite chair.

Eventually, she came to the image she had been looking for: her father, holding Toshiko in his arms, while behind them the fireworks exploded in the skies over Osaka and the decorated boats sailed down the Dojima River.

Toshiko touched the photograph, and smiled.

Gwen Cooper slid the key into the lock, pulled it back about a millimetre, pressed it to the left, and then turned it. That was the trick. The lock clicked, and she opened the door.

Rhys was on the sofa, watching television.

'You're home, then,' he said in a flat monotone.

'Yeah,' said Gwen, hanging up her coat before joining him. She sat next to him, and waited a moment before speaking again.

'I'm sorry,' she said. 'I'm sorry about the food, and I'm sorry about the sofa, and… I'm just sorry.'

'You're sorry about the sofa?' said Rhys, sounding genuinely surprised.

'Yeah,' said Gwen. 'I've been thinking about it, and it's not *that* bad.'

'Not that bad?' asked Rhys. 'You said it was the sort of thing Jordan and Peter Andre would buy.'

'Yeah,' said Gwen. 'But it's *just* a sofa. D'you know what I mean?'

Rhys laughed. 'It's OK,' he said. 'I've been thinking about it, and you're right. I mean… If *they'd* buy it…'

Gwen laughed too. 'So…' she said. 'The spag bol?'

'I'll put it on now,' he said. 'Anyway… Spag bol always tastes better if you leave it for a bit.'

Gwen held Rhys's hand and squeezed it gently.

'I love you,' she said.

'I love you, too,' said Rhys.

The SUV drove out along the waterfront, past the old Norwegian church and the cluster of modern buildings. It pulled up in front of a row of enormous apartment buildings, each one with a balcony overlooking Cardiff Bay. Some of the lights inside the apartments were still on, some were lit up a flickering blue by unseen television screens.

Jack Harkness stepped out of the vehicle and opened the back doors. Inside, resting on the back seat, was the Orb. He lifted it out, groaning with the weight, and kicked the SUV's door shut before carrying the Orb to the water's edge.

Forty years ago, there had been no apartment buildings here. Forty years ago, this place had been home to a row of warehouses, the largest of which, Hamilton's Sugar, had stood right on the edge of the dock. The warehouses were gone now; even those which had survived that night had been bulldozed and replaced by apartment buildings and hotels.

Jack gazed down at the black surface of the sea. He felt an affinity with the ocean, as if it were a kindred spirit. The knowledge that every drop of water had always been a drop of water, practically since the stars were formed. Water was infinite and immortal. He lifted the Orb to his chest, and looked at it one last time – the unfathomable engravings on its surface, etched billions of years ago by unknown hands with unknown tools. It could have been a thing of beauty, in another life, perhaps, an object to sit behind glass in a museum. But not now.

Jack hurled the Orb into the sea and it hit the water with an enormous splash, sinking quickly out of sight. It was against the rules, of course. The Orb should have been returned to Basement D-4, another half-forgotten relic in the Torchwood Archive, but Jack didn't care. It was history, and he was thinking of the future. And the past and the future were different worlds.

Most of the time.

ACKNOWLEDGEMENTS

Thanks to all those at BBC Wales and BBC Books who set me on the path to writing this book: Edward Russell, Gary Russell, Mathew Clayton, and my editor and oracle, Steve Tribe. Thanks also to the friends who kept me sane and in my happy place while I was writing it, especially Benny Flambards (aka Lord Tinlegs) who listened to the book, chapter by chapter, as it was being written, and supplied the tea and biscuits. And, lastly, to my aunties, the Gait sisters, for their info on 1950s nursing practices.

With one or two alterations, the story 'The Land of Perpetual Life' has been adapted from the Japanese fairy tale 'The Story of the Man Who Did Not Wish to Die', as included in the volume *Japanese Fairy Tales* by Yei Theodora Ozaki.

Also available from BBC Books

TORCHWOOD
ANOTHER LIFE
Peter Anghelides

ISBN 978 0 563 48653 4
UK £6.99 US$11.99/$14.99 CDN

Thick black clouds are blotting out the skies over Cardiff. As twenty-four inches of rain fall in twenty-four hours, the city centre's drainage system collapses. The capital's homeless are being murdered, their mutilated bodies left lying in the soaked streets around the Blaidd Drwg nuclear facility.

Tracked down by Torchwood, the killer calmly drops eight storeys to his death. But the killings don't stop. Their investigations lead Jack Harkness, Gwen Cooper and Toshiko Sato to a monster in a bathroom, a mystery at an army base and a hunt for stolen nuclear fuel rods. Meanwhile, Owen Harper goes missing from the Hub, when a game in *Second Reality* leads him to an old girlfriend...

Something is coming, forcing its way through the Rift, straight into Cardiff Bay.

Featuring Captain Jack Harkness as played by John Barrowman, with Gwen Cooper, Owen Harper, Toshiko Sato and Ianto Jones as played by Eve Myles, Burn Gorman, Naoki Mori and Gareth David-Lloyd, in the hit series created by Russell T Davies for BBC Television.

T O R C H W O O D
BORDER PRINCES
Dan Abnett

ISBN 978 0 563 48654 1
UK £6.99 US$11.99/$14.99 CDN

The End of the World began on a Thursday night in October, just after eight in the evening…

The Amok is driving people out of their minds, turning them into zombies and causing riots in the streets. A solitary diner leaves a Cardiff restaurant, his mission to protect the Principal leading him to a secret base beneath a water tower. Everyone has a headache, there's something in Davey Morgan's shed, and the church of St Mary-in-the-Dust, demolished in 1840, has reappeared – though it's not due until 2011. Torchwood seem to be out of their depth. What will all this mean for the romance between Torchwood's newest members?

Captain Jack Harkness has something more to worry about: an alarm, an early warning, given to mankind and held – inert – by Torchwood for 108 years. And now it's flashing. Something is coming. Or something is already here.

Featuring Captain Jack Harkness as played by John Barrowman, with Gwen Cooper, Owen Harper, Toshiko Sato and Ianto Jones as played by Eve Myles, Burn Gorman, Naoki Mori and Gareth David-Lloyd, in the hit series created by Russell T Davies for BBC Television.

When Torchwood track an energy surge to a Cardiff nightclub, the team finds the police are already at the scene. Five teenagers have died in a fight, and lying among the bodies is an unfamiliar device. Next morning, they discover the corpse of a Weevil, its face and neck eaten away, seemingly by human teeth. And on the streets of Cardiff, an ordinary woman with an extraordinary hunger is attacking people and eating her victims.

The job of a lifetime it might be, but working for Torchwood is putting big strains on Gwen's relationship with Rhys. While she decides to spice up their love life with the help of alien technology, Rhys decides it's time to sort himself out – better music, healthier food, lose some weight. Luckily, a friend has mentioned Doctor Scotus's weight-loss clinic…

Featuring Captain Jack Harkness as played by John Barrowman, with Gwen Cooper, Owen Harper, Toshiko Sato and Ianto Jones as played by Eve Myles, Burn Gorman, Naoki Mori and Gareth David-Lloyd, in the hit series created by Russell T Davies for BBC Television.

Dr Bob Strong's GP surgery has been treating a lot of coughs and colds recently, far more than is normal for the time of year. Bob thinks there's something up but he can't think what. He seems to have caught it himself, whatever it is – he's starting to cough badly and there are flecks of blood in his hanky.

Saskia Harden has been found on a number of occasions submerged in ponds or canals but alive and seemingly none the worse for wear. Saskia is not on any files, except in the medical records at Dr Strong's GP practice.

But Torchwood's priorities lie elsewhere: investigating ghostly apparitions in South Wales, they have found a dead body. It's old and in an advanced state of decay. And it is still able to talk.

And what it is saying is 'Water hag'…

Featuring Captain Jack Harkness as played by John Barrowman, with Gwen Cooper, Owen Harper, Toshiko Sato and Ianto Jones as played by Eve Myles, Burn Gorman, Naoki Mori and Gareth David-Lloyd, in the hit series created by Russell T Davies for BBC Television.

Also available from BBC Books

T O R C H W O O D
THE TWILIGHT STREETS
Gary Russell

ISBN 978 1 84607 439 4
UK £6.99 US$11.99/$14.99 CDN

There's a part of the city that no one much goes to, a collection of rundown old houses and gloomy streets. No one stays there long, and no one can explain why – something's not quite right there.

Now the Council is renovating the district, and a new company is overseeing the work. There will be street parties and events to show off the newly gentrified neighbourhood: clowns and face-painters for the kids, magicians for the adults – the street entertainers of Cardiff, out in force.

None of this is Torchwood's problem. Until Toshiko recognises the sponsor of the street parties: Bilis Manger.

Now there is something for Torchwood to investigate. But Captain Jack Harkness has never been able to get into the area; it makes him physically ill to go near it. Without Jack's help, Torchwood must face the darker side of urban Cardiff alone...

Featuring Captain Jack Harkness as played by John Barrowman, with Gwen Cooper, Owen Harper, Toshiko Sato and Ianto Jones as played by Eve Myles, Burn Gorman, Naoki Mori and Gareth David-Lloyd, in the hit series created by Russell T Davies for BBC Television.